Long Road to Survival:

The Prepper Series
Book 2

ISBN: 978-1-926456-08-9

Dedication

A special thank you to H. Rossi, Craig and Leslie for the time you spent reading through and commenting on early versions of the manuscript. I'd also like to thank my editor RJ for helping to add that mirror finish to the final draft. And finally a word of gratitude to fans of the series. Without you, none of this would be possible.

Long Road to Survival (Book 2)

America continues to teeter on the brink of collapse after terrorists detonate black-market nukes from container ships.

With deadly clouds of radiation swooping in from the wasteland of American port cities, Paul Edwards and his father-in-law Buck seek shelter in a spectacular government bunker, the likes of which has never been seen.

They've succeeded in finding safety from the threats outside, but in a world without rules, trust can be a dangerous thing.

Recap of book one

After a devastating terrorist attack, former rock star Paul Edwards and his cranky father-in-law Buck Baker put aside their differences and journey a thousand miles to Atlanta in the hopes of saving their loved ones. What should have been a long drive becomes a life-or-death struggle when the two men are set upon by a gang of recently escaped criminals. But reaching Paul's wife Susan and his daughter Autumn is only half the battle. With deadly radiation about to envelop Atlanta, they take the only viable option open to them—an invitation to a government bunker. There they will wait for the radiation to pass. It's a safe place, populated with fellow Americans. What could possibly go wrong?

Chapter 1

Three days ago

The traffic along I-95 between Baltimore and Washington, DC ground to a standstill and Speaker of the House Edmund Perkins wondered if he'd ever make it back to Capitol Hill. The weather outside the protected confines of his Mercedes S600 armoured limousine was well on its way to becoming a typical southeastern summer day, which was to say that it was hot, muggy and made Perkins thankful for the breeze from the air conditioning brushing his face.

The stifling heat outside reminded him of the story they used to tell new interns—that Washington had been built on a swamp—an analogy that seemed particularly relevant to many nowadays who had grown tired of the current political climate in Washington. Unfortunately, the story wasn't true. Only about two percent of the city was swamp land, and yet for years the story had persisted. Perkins supposed it spoke to an observation made by Mark Twain more than a hundred years before that one should never let the truth get in the way of a good story.

Sitting next to him, Mark Thomson, his thin and meticulous assistant, thumbed through a daily planner. If Perkins was the helm, then Thomson was the rudder that kept the ship pointed in the right direction.

"We're not gonna make the meeting," Thomson said, tapping his brown loafer.

Perkins pushed a button on the side console, lowering the tinted window which sealed off the limo's back seat. A pair of gunmetal-black eyes stared back at him through the rear view.

"What can I do for you, sir?" Johnson asked. At well over two hundred pounds, the man might just as well have also been Perkins' bodyguard. It certainly would have eliminated the need for the black SUV behind them, carrying the two Secret Service agents tasked with his protection.

"When do you expect we'll arrive?" Perkins asked. "I've got an important meeting with Senator Janice Grotz at…" He looked at Thomson, who mouthed the time.

"Three."

Johnson's right hand went into the air. "If I could turn this here limo into a chopper, I'd say no more time than it takes to drain a Scotch on the rocks."

Perkins grinned. That was Johnson's way of telling him to have a drink and enjoy the ride. If Johnson only knew. There was more on Perkins' plate right now than his driver could ever understand. Besides, Perkins didn't drink, not anymore. He'd been dry for close to twenty years now. Ever since coming under the wing of Victor Van Buren, the man who had made all of this possible.

The thought of Van Buren prompted Perkins to check his phone. The old man was supposed to call. It wasn't like him to break his word.

Just then a blinding flash washed over everything. Cars ahead of them slowed, some swerved and crashed into the cement median. On the other side of the highway, all traffic had come to a complete stop. Afterward, Perkins would remember the look of horror on their faces, as though the Rapture had begun.

Then he saw it for himself, reflected in the windshield of an oncoming eighteen-wheeler, and Perkins understood their fear. They were watching a mushroom cloud rising from what had once been Baltimore, a city that now likely resembled something out of the Old Testament itself, Sodom and Gomorrah. Pulsing out from the city, the shockwave swept over the traffic, bursting windows and tossing cars aside like children's toys. A single thought had time to flash through Perkins' mind before it hit: the attack had come too early.

The limo was lying with its belly to the darkening sky when Perkins came to, a stinging pain at his temple. He touched the area with his hand and it came away red. The bulletproof windows had resisted the blast wave, but the car had been tossed around like a leaf in the wind. On top of that, shards of glass from the shattered divider had sprayed him in the face. Next to him Thomson, his eyes open, stared blankly into space. Reaching over with shaky fingers, Perkins felt for a pulse, knowing full well he wouldn't find one.

A moan from the front seat drew his attention.

"Johnson, you okay?"

"I hope you got the license plate of the truck that hit us."

Johnson was being held upside down by his seatbelt. Perkins, on the other hand, was lying on the ceiling next to Thomson's dead body.

After opening the limo door, the Speaker of the House pushed his way out of the vehicle and into a hellish landscape. The highway was strewn with wrecked cars and dead Americans. It seemed unimaginable that anyone could live through such a disaster and yet, amidst the clouds of smoke and the smell of burning rubber, the vague shapes of human figures stumbled around. Most of them were moving slowly—as if out on a leisurely Sunday stroll—and he recognized right away that they were in shock. A handful of others had sprung into action, wrestling against twisted car doors in order to free those trapped in the chaos.

That made him think of Johnson and he made his way to the driver's side door. Grasping the metal handle, Perkins glanced behind him for just a moment and his pulse quickened at the sight of the mushroom cloud, a towering column rising high into the atmosphere, already beginning to lose its shape. It was growing fatter and starting to look more like a swollen finger. Soon the fallout—radioactive debris sucked high into the air with the initial detonation—would begin descending back to earth. In another thirty minutes, these people were as good as dead.

He wrestled with the car door, his nostrils filled with smoke and his arms as heavy as lead pipes. His Brioni suit was shredded, giving him the appearance of a character from Looney Tunes who'd lit a trick cigar.

Finally the door swung open to reveal Johnson still suspended upside down. The driver's arms were touching the ceiling, his head moving back and forth as he spoke. Perkins ducked in to undo the seatbelt and

4

swore it sounded as though the man were praying. For reasons he wasn't free to explain, Perkins felt responsible and reassured the driver that he'd be just fine. But the latch on the seatbelt wasn't releasing. The weight of Johnson's robust body was putting too much pressure on the mechanism. He would need to find a knife and cut the belt to have any hope of saving the man. Right about that time, a helicopter approached.

It was an unmarked black chopper and it circled twice before setting down in a field beside the highway. A door slid open and three men in suits wielding MP5 submachine guns emerged. The sight brought to mind his own security detail and Perkins scanned the devastation before spotting their black SUV. Or what was left of it.

The men in suits arrived a minute later.

"Mr. Speaker, we need you to come with us."

They were Secret Service, he could tell from the suits they wore as well as the calm, emotionless way they addressed him.

"Not without Johnson," Perkins said, motioning to his trapped driver. "And there are two more of your men in that crumpled SUV over there."

They glanced over their shoulders and then back at him. "No one else but you, sir," the first one said. The man behind him had swapped his weapon for a Geiger counter which was clicking away.

"Then I won't go."

The head agent took Perkins by the arm. "Our orders were clear. Now either you come willingly or we can hogtie and carry you off."

The blood drained from Perkins' face. He stared for a moment at the survivors around him, struggling to help one another. None of them knew it would all be in vain. It wasn't supposed to happen, not like this.

The Secret Service agent tightened his grip and began pulling Perkins away as the Speaker gave in and agreed to go.

Johnson was reaching for him. "Don't leave me, please don't leave me."

But like much of life these last few years, Perkins didn't have a choice. Already he knew Van Buren would hear about his refusal to leave. His benefactor would be displeased but Perkins wasn't sure if he cared anymore. He had allowed the man to cross the Rubicon and Perkins was beginning to wonder if they hadn't made a terrible mistake.

The Secret Service chopper flew over the capital on its way to one of a half-dozen bunkers that ringed Washington, DC. Carryovers from the Cold War, many of the bunkers had either been put on the chopping block or dismantled over the years. But no more than six months ago, all that had changed. With secret black-budget funding, the underground installations had been hurriedly brought back online.

As they'd approached the city from a distance, Perkins was amazed at how calm and intact the capital was. Especially considering the mushroom cloud behind them, long since distorted by the wind into a misshapen column of smoke and ash.

It was only as they reached the Potomac that Perkins spotted the first signs of trouble. The freeways leaving the city were jammed with the vehicles of those trying to flee. By far the largest line stretched from I-66 toward the interior of the country and presumably away from the coastal cities, several of which had been reduced to radioactive wastelands.

Not long after the chopper touched down outside of an ageing factory. In its entire history, Discount Auto Parts hadn't produced a single fuel filter or brake pad. Even though transport trucks could be seen coming and going on a regular basis, the structure was nothing more than a cover for Continuity of Government Bunker Five, an underground structure designed to house a portion of the legislative branch of the government in the event of a serious threat. Other strong points outside the city would house other government agencies—one the Pentagon, another Homeland Security and a third the FBI, CIA and NSA.

A group of men in dark suits approached the helicopter, bent slightly at the waist, avoiding the blades still rotating overhead.

Without saying a word, the men led Perkins from the chopper toward a nondescript door. On the wall next to the factory entrance was a sign which read: *1856 days accident-free.*

"What a track record," Perkins observed. "Even if she isn't real."

The Secret Service agent next to him grinned as he punched a code into a keypad and pulled open the door. "You should see our benefits package."

No sooner had they entered than a voice rang out. "Oh, God, Edmund, your face. What happened?"

"Had a little car trouble," he replied, reaching for cuts on his left cheek where glass from the divider had struck his face.

The voice belonged to Senator Janice Grotz from Connecticut. In her late fifties and skinny as a pole, Janice was as smart as they came. With five ex-husbands behind her, she was also known around the Hill as the Black Widow.

"Those bastards really got us this time, didn't they?" Her tiny hands were balled into fists.

"I guess I don't need to tell you I won't make our meeting today," Perkins quipped as he and his entourage of Secret Service agents pushed past her.

She ignored his ill-timed joke, calling after him instead. "Have you heard about the president?"

Perkins stopped and spun on his heels, hopeful. "No, I haven't."

Her eyes fell. "We only just found out ourselves. He's dead, Edmund. Was in New York addressing the United Nations when the city was destroyed." She was visibly shaken and fighting back the tears.

"What about the vice president?" Perkins asked her, feigning grief.

"Alive," Janice replied, "but barely. He was in Los Angeles. He's unconscious, maybe even in a coma. But we haven't heard anything else." She paused, her features becoming set. "I guess as Speaker of the House that makes you acting president."

Senator Grotz's words were still ringing in Perkins' ears as the elevator descended to sublevel two, opening onto the situation room. A bank of monitors on the far wall showed maps of the United States and the cities along both coasts that had been destroyed. Agents and analysts scrambled to organize rescue teams tasked with helping the wounded and searching for survivors. So much needed to be done. Portable mortuaries needed setting up. The Emergency Alert System needed to begin broadcasting messages to Americans on how to stay safe from the fallout. The list was never-ending.

The faces of representatives from government agencies headquartered in other secret bunkers around the Capitol appeared on each of the screens. They were waiting for direction, for a leader who could help them find a way out of this mess. If the president or vice president were around, this was where they would be. It wasn't long before all of the screens were filled.

An analyst wearing a headset swivelled to face Perkins. "We're ready to begin."

"Not just yet," Perkins replied. "First, get me an encrypted line to Sugarloaf Mountain."

Victor Van Buren sounded euphoric as he answered the line. "I would normally be cross you took so long to report in, but under the circumstances I find myself in a rather forgiving mood. Are you alone?"

"For now," Perkins told him, trying to calm the rising panic in his voice. "There's a room full of people next door waiting for me to act presidential."

"Then all is unfolding as we intended."

"Not exactly."

Van Buren's smooth voice became icy. "What do you mean?"

"Vice President Trindle. He's still alive."

"Really? He must've been right at the edge of the blast radius," Van Buren said almost to himself.

"But he may be in a coma," Perkins assured him. "At least that's what I've heard so far."

Van Buren paused, presumably to savor the Earl Grey he was always drinking. "Then you'll need to make sure that he never wakes up."

Perkins went to respond, but the line was already dead.

Chapter 2

Present

Paul Edwards opened his sleepy eyes as the strangely shaped mountain came into view. From its flattened crest rose a crop of tightly packed trees and his first impression was that it resembled a stumpy loaf of bread. Rubbing at his eyes, he couldn't help wondering whether he was still asleep.

"Looks kinda like an old man wearing a bad toupee," Susan observed from behind the wheel of Buck's Hummer. The convoy leaving Atlanta had pulled over somewhere outside of Memphis and they'd swapped places. During their race south to rescue Susan and Autumn, the two men hadn't slept more than a handful of hours and before long the exhaustion had started catching up with them.

Paul glanced into the back seat to find Buck out cold, a patch of blood staining his bandaged wound. The young soldier who'd talked his commanding officer into allowing them to come along—Paul thought his name was Brett—had said they were heading for a bunker somewhere outside the city. But they'd already driven through three states over the course of several hours.

As the long column of military and civilian vehicles drew closer to the mountain, Paul could see it stood in the middle of the lake, like a medieval castle surrounded by a deep moat. A pontoon bridge spanned the waterway and as the first vehicles began to cross, Paul was suddenly sure they were about to enter the most secure piece of real estate in the country.

Autumn leaned forward from the backseat, staring through the windshield wide-eyed. "Are we there yet?"

"Seems that way," Paul replied. "How's your grandpa doing?"

She touched the side of his neck with the pads of her fingers and waited. "He's got a pulse." Autumn's eyes rose to a place just over Paul's shoulder. "Holy cow!"

Metal clanged as the locking bolts on a giant vault door opened slowly before them. The lead Humvees entered followed by the rest in line. For a moment, Susan hesitated. Several of the civilian vehicles behind her beeped.

"What is it, honey?" Paul asked his wife.

She clutched the wheel. "Nothing important," she replied.

If their many years of marriage had taught Paul anything, it was that 'nothing' always meant 'something'. Susan nudged the Hummer's front tires onto the pontoon bridge and drove them across. "Besides," she finally said. "We need to get ourselves out of this radiation as soon as possible."

"We do," Paul added. "Especially before too many rads mutate Buck into a grouchy old coot."

11

"Dad, I think we're a little late for that," Autumn replied, grinning nervously.

Almost on cue, Buck rolled over and began to snore. The three burst into fits of laughter which continued until the vault door closed behind them with a thunderous boom.

Chapter 3

The row of military and civilian vehicles traveled down a dimly lit tunnel into the heart of the mountain. Reflectors embedded into the asphalt as well as small cage lights mounted on the passageway's walls were the sole source of illumination.

Paul stared ahead as a new light in the distance appeared. Somehow seeing it eased the tightness building inside his chest. He cracked the window slightly and caught a whiff of car exhaust mixed with concrete. It almost felt like they had entered the underground parking for some shopping mall, a perception that was only reinforced when they came to an open area.

On one side in neat rows were dozens, perhaps hundreds of vehicles of all kinds: cars, trucks, family vans and even a few motor homes. But it was what he spotted on the other side that brought all of that tension roaring back. Orange, black and yellow tents bearing biological, chemical and radiological symbols. People from the parking lot were being herded into long sorting lines.

Somehow, Paul had just assumed that their admittance was a foregone conclusion, as though the word of Autumn's soldier friend Brett was more than enough. What would they do if they were turned away? Head back into the growing cloud of radiation that was surely not far behind them? No, the idea seemed unthinkable. He and Buck had braved countless dangers as well as a group of deranged ex-Army thugs in order to rescue Susan and Autumn. They'd come too far to find safety only to be turned away at the last minute.

After finding a spot for the Hummer, the three got out. An unconscious Buck would need to be carried by stretcher into the bunker's medical facility. A mix of weary soldiers and civilians headed toward the tents. Everyone was clearly worn out from the long journey. Paul waved a hand at Brett, beckoning him over.

"Dad, what are you doing?" Autumn scolded him. "I can't let him see my hair like this."

"You want your grandfather to die from his wounds?" Paul shot back.

Brett arrived and Paul asked him about finding some medical personnel to help. He nodded and jogged off.

A few moments later, as people continued to stream past them in the parking area, two men in hazmat suits arrived pushing a stretcher.

"You folks are gonna need to line up for processing," one of them said, pointing to the tents Paul had watched with a hint of dread on the way in.

"Where are we?" Susan asked, looking around at the high-vaulted ceilings and the throngs of people. "What is this place?"

"This is the Ark."

They helped to load Buck on the stretcher before he was carted away.

14

"Thanks for the info," Paul replied under his breath. "The Ark. That explains a lot."

They followed the crowd and settled into a place in line. At last they came to a table where a black officer in a hazmat suit was seated.

"Can I see your ID, please?" he asked in a muffled, hollow voice.

Paul stuck a hand in his back pocket and his heart iced over with panic. His wallet was gone, stolen by Finch's men during the ambush at the gas station.

The officer looked annoyed. "No ID?"

"My wallet was stolen."

Autumn and Susan laid their driver's licenses on the table.

"This is my husband," Susan told him as he studied each card. "We're trying to get home to Nebraska."

"You're the last group to arrive," he told them. "If you're admitted, you won't be heading home until the radiation clears."

"And if we're not admitted?" Paul asked, not sure he wanted to hear the answer.

"Then you'll be escorted out by one of the MPs."

The man passed a scanner over each of the two IDs.

"Looking for fakes?" Autumn inquired politely.

He handed them back. "Taking a picture for our database." He motioned to Paul. "You, sir, are gonna need to fill out a series of forms. But first we need to check you for contaminants." Pushing up out of his seat, the officer spread the newcomers a few feet apart from one another and produced a dosimeter which he waved back and forth in front of Autumn and Susan. He then did the same to Paul. The machine let out a loud squeal, indicating radiation exposure.

"I'm sorry, sir, but I can't let you in," he told them.

Paul's chest seized painfully. Beside him, another man was being told the same thing. The man began to argue

15

and two MPs appeared and took him by the arm, leading him back to the parking area.

Paul swung back to the officer before him.

"Sir… Did you hear what I said?"

"That can't be," Paul stammered. "I tested each of us on the road and we were all fine. I mean, we've been exposed a little bit, but surely no more than anyone else who's just arrived."

Two more MPs emerged from one of the tents and headed his way.

Paul swallowed hard. "Maybe your machine's not working properly."

"I'm sorry, sir."

"Just try it again, would you?"

Another officer with deep-set eyes wearing a hazmat suit showed up.

"What's the problem here?"

The first officer showed him the dosimeter. "His reading's way off the chart."

"There must be a mistake," Paul told them. The concern was starting to show on Susan and Autumn's faces.

"I'm sorry, but the dosimeter doesn't make mistakes," the second man said.

"Maybe we should leave," Susan cut in.

"What about Grandpa Buck?" Autumn asked.

Paul had contemplated what might happen if all of them had been denied entry to the bunker, but he hadn't considered the possibility that only one of them might not make it.

"You two stay with Buck," he told them. "I'll go out on my own and make my way to Nebraska."

The mere suggestion seemed to mortify his wife and daughter. Susan turned to the officer holding the dosimeter, fighting back the tears. "For heaven's sake, will you just try it one more time?" She wasn't getting anything. "Please."

The officer's resolve began to waver. Resetting the handheld machine, he waved it in front of Paul's body and held the view screen up to his colleague.

"My apologies, ma'am, looks like your husband is clean." He waved his hand. "Please proceed to the orange tent for decontamination."

Paul nearly collapsed with relief.

They did as they were told, Paul feeling as though his heart was about to explode in his chest. Autumn clutched his arm.

"I can't believe they nearly kicked you out," his daughter said.

Susan nodded. "Makes you wonder about the poor guy at the table next to ours." She turned to Paul, who was still upset.

"Not only was I nearly expelled to my death," he said, "he had the nerve to apologise to *you*."

Susan smiled. "It's over, honey. Stop fretting or you're gonna give yourself a coronary."

The humiliation, however, was only just beginning. From here they were forced to undress, their clothes placed into plastic bags and tossed into a cart marked *Incineration.* Cold and with nothing to shield themselves, they were sent one by one into decontamination showers and sprayed with an awful-smelling liquid before being rinsed with freezing water. Emerging on the other side, they were handed a towel and escorted into one of several improvised medical booths. There they were instructed to bend over while they received a shot in their rear end.

Paul squinted with the pain. "What was that for?" he howled.

"An inoculation," an overweight and bored-looking nurse replied before shooing him away and waving over the next in line.

Finally they came to a final tent where each of them was handed a bundle of clothing and given a small dressing room to change in. Paul did as he was told and emerged at the same time as Susan and Autumn. The look on his daughter's face was priceless. Despite having suffered the humiliation of being stripped, showered and inoculated in the behind, the thought of wearing a beige tunic and trousers was somehow too much.

"I look like something out of a Kanye West fashion show," Autumn cried in despair.

"We all do, honey," Susan said, curling an arm around her daughter. "But our stuff's being burned."

"I kinda like it." Paul smiled, looking down at himself. "Reminds me of my hippy days."

Susan threw him a funny look. "You were never a hippy."

"No, but I almost was. Right before I landed with The Wanderers."

"Please, Dad. If I hear another story about how you used to be in a rock band I'm gonna run screaming into a radiation cloud. The Rolling Stones or the Beatles, that woulda been cool, but The Wanderers?"

Ahead of them lay a final set of impressive-looking doors. Gleaming steel, they stood open and welcoming. Standing next to them with warm smiles were a man and woman in military uniforms.

"Welcome to the Ark," they said, almost in unison.

They reminded Paul of the way flight attendants addressed passengers as they entered a plane and for a moment it made him forget about the legions of citizens trapped outside of these impenetrable walls, many of them suffering and dying. Paul and his family were among the lucky ones. They'd lived through the worst of it. Made it to safety. The gravest dangers were now far behind them. From here on in, things could only get better.

Chapter 4

That growing sense of euphoria continued as they were led by a young man in plain clothes to the living quarters, which he referred to as Ark One. His name was Craig, he told them. Six months ago he'd been an intern for a large government contractor and today he was working as human resources officer in a bunker in Sugarloaf Mountain.

"Who woulda guessed?" he joked, his eyes twinkling.

They entered an enormous corrugated tunnel and Craig's voice echoed as he explained they were about to take the bunker's internal tram system. No fewer than twenty feet in diameter, the passage connected the three main branches of the complex, Arks One, Two and Three.

"The bunker gets its power from the Greers Ferry Dam," Craig told them as they stood on the platform. "But every so often the power goes down and we're forced to walk between sections or through the Park."

"The Park?" Paul asked.

Craig grinned. "You'll see."

"How far is it?" Susan asked, glancing down with concern at the plastic Croc-like shoes they'd been given to wear.

"Oh, not too far. Maybe half a mile."

Paul caught the sound of a subway train approaching just as a group of newcomers fell in line behind them fresh from the decontamination process.

"Welcome," Craig greeted them.

They looked worn out, some even upset. The entire procedure was unpleasant and even embarrassing—the inoculation in his backside was still smarting—but it sure beat the alternative.

A three-car train glided into the station on rows of rubber wheels. The doors swooshed open and everyone on the platform entered. Others were onboard, many dressed just like them. Paul nodded and they returned the gesture. In many cases their clothes showed signs of wear, which told him they must have arrived sometime over the last few days.

A woman's voice came over the intercom.

"Next station: Ark One. Living quarters. Mess hall. Rest and recreation."

"How many people live here?" he asked Craig, looking around at the mostly filled subway cars.

"You folks are all curious," Craig told the group of newcomers. "I get it, but you have no need to worry. In time, all of your questions will be answered."

If Buck were here, Paul knew he'd be telling this kid that time was now. But unlike his impatient and cranky father-in-law, Paul figured the best thing right now was to go with the flow and trust in the process, no matter how strange or foreign it might seem.

"The truth is," Craig whispered to him, "I've already overstepped my bounds."

"What do you mean?"

"Well, my boss is the one who'll be giving you your orientation. If she tells you anything I've already covered, just play dumb, will you?" He flashed that million-dollar smile.

"Sure thing, Craig."

It appeared that even in heaven, bureaucracy was alive and well.

The living quarters were impressive, a veritable multi-story apartment complex rising up from inside the mountain. The room Paul's family would share was little more than a glorified dormitory. Stacked along both walls were sets of bunk beds. To the left of the entrance was a quaint sitting area with a table and chairs along with a desk and desktop computer. The screen was black except for the words 'ACCESS CODE:' in bold print. Their policy of one family per room, as Craig explained, made all the difference.

"Well, it's less Ritz Carlton and more Motel 8," Paul said, trying out the mattress on the bottom bunk and finding it hard. "But it could be worse."

"Hey, look at this," Susan said, pointing. A digital screen made to look like a window showed a field of tall prairie grass, blowing in the wind.

"Cool," Paul said, fluffing the freshly pressed pillow.

"You think we have access to the internet?" Autumn asked.

"I hope not," Paul replied.

How funny the world was. The country had suffered an unspeakable tragedy. Millions of lives lost, the power grid down, in turn disconnecting the country from the gadgets and gizmos that formed the backbone of our technological addiction. And while the first part was enough to make a person shudder, the death—temporary or not—of cell phones and the internet had brought his family closer together.

The drive from Atlanta had been the first time in forever he and Autumn had had a real conversation. Not the distracted words between incoming texts that had replaced actual human interaction. There was more than enough to be sad about, no doubt about it. But as with any cataclysmic change, glimmers of light could always be found.

Chapter 5

The next morning, they boarded the tram bound for Ark Two, the structure which housed the science and engineering departments as well as the infirmary. When they arrived, they found an area that was bright and modern with pristine white walls. A handful of medical staff criss-crossed from one patient to another. Most were other civilians in beige tunics suffering from a range of minor ailments. Judging from the saline IV drips plugged into people's arms, the majority were battling dehydration. A handful were members of the military and even fewer were men in dark suits.

A booming voice drew everyone's attention.

"Get that dang thing away from me."

"Sir, would you please cooperate," a male nurse could be heard saying. "You've just had an operation."

"Come one step closer and you'll be the one needing a doctor."

Paul caught the knowing expression on Susan's face. "Sounds like Dad's awake."

A blue light blinked above the doorway to one of the rooms and the three of them rushed in that direction. Two nurses pushed past them.

They entered to find Buck backed into a corner, dressed in little more than a blue patient gown. The nurses must have been in the middle of giving him his inoculation when he began fighting them off.

"What'd you animals do with my clothes?" he bellowed.

"The same thing we had to do with everyone else's clothes, sir," a female nurse shouted. "We burned them."

"Buck," Paul yelled, hoping the forcefulness in his voice might help get through to his father-in-law. "These people are here to help you. Take the shot like the rest of us."

Buck's eyes darted around the room. "Where the heck are we?"

"Dad, we're at a government bunker called the Ark," Susan said, trying to soothe him. "Paul's right. These people aren't going to hurt you."

"Yeah, that's what you think."

"He hates needles," Susan told the nurses gathered in a half-circle around her father.

The head nurse held up what looked like a plastic gun. "Mr. Baker, this is an auto-injector. It shoots the inoculation directly into the body."

Paul nodded. "Your backside won't hurt for more than a day or two."

Susan elbowed him in the ribs. "You're not helping." She turned to the nurses. "Why don't you let me see if I can help."

As his daughter approached, Buck's arms fell to his sides, his face returning to a measure of sanity. Slowly, Buck pulled the drawstrings of his robe and tied them

25

together. With the awkward balance of a man who'd come awake in the middle of the night, Buck moved to the examination table and sat down.

"You're in remarkable shape for a man your age," the head nurse told him. "But what you need now, Mr. Baker, is some rest and relaxation."

Buck seemed to agree. Susan put her hand on his good shoulder.

"Now, roll over onto your stomach and undo the back of your robe," the nurse said in a soothing voice.

Buck hesitated.

"Go ahead, Dad. You're okay."

The head nurse addressed Paul and Autumn. "You two can stay as well to hold his hand if you'd like."

Paul laughed. "If I see whatever that robe is hiding, I may be scarred for life."

"You will when you see what a real man looks like," Buck shouted, lying face down on the examining table.

Just then a beautiful woman appeared in the doorway and everyone in the room, including Buck, turned to watch her.

In her mid-forties and stunning, the woman was dressed in a slim-fitting grey jacket and skirt. With skin the color of almond milk and her dark hair tied up in a bun, she was breathtaking. Despite her beauty, there was something about this woman that made it clear she wasn't to be trifled with. Her gaze shifted from Paul, to Susan, then to Autumn. "Ava Monroe," she told them. "I'm Director Van Buren's assistant. The three of you need to come with me."

They looked from one to another with a growing sense of unease. Were they in trouble?

If ever Buck had reason to jump around and create a scene it was now, but the old guy's expression had changed. Gone was the suspicion from a second ago. Buck's face was strangely gentle, and Paul couldn't shake the impression that his father-in-law had just experienced one of those rarest of emotions: love at first sight.

Chapter 6

They were standing outside the infirmary in a brilliantly lit hallway that looked like something from a spaceship.

"There's no need to worry," Ava told Paul, pressing flat the seams of her skirt. "You and your family are not in trouble. I'm simply here to give you a tour of the facility."

The air escaped his lungs along with his anxiety.

"Our own private tour?" Susan asked with a touch of suspicion. His wife's striking red hair was tangled and unkempt and Paul could see she was feeling self-conscious in the company of a woman this beautiful. "What'd we do to deserve the VIP treatment?"

Ava's lips nearly curled into a grin, but didn't. "Believe me, none of you are being given special treatment. As we make our way through the Ark's various facilities we'll be seeing lots of other groups. Mr. Victor Van Buren thought that since we'll all be spending some time together, it was best that our civilian guests be shown around."

"Van Buren?" Paul said. "He run this place?"

"Think of him as the appointed mayor."

Susan shook her head. "What you really mean to do is show us where we can and can't go."

Autumn tugged at her mother's sleeve. "Mom, be nice."

Ava paused. "Please let me remind you, Mrs. Edwards, that you and your family are currently in a top-secret government facility. Our instructions were to seal the blast doors and leave civilians on the other side and yet the director defied protocol and did exactly the opposite. And you're right, some parts of the facility are strictly off-limits, but that's to prevent sensitive information being leaked to the very people who may wish to destroy us."

The muscles in Susan's face settled. "You're absolutely right. Please accept my apology."

"Hey, this whole situation is messed up," Paul chimed in. "We've been through a lot in the last few days and tensions are high. We don't mean any disrespect."

"And none was taken," Ava replied. "Whether we like it or not, we're all in this together. Part of that means learning to trust one another." She motioned to Buck, who had wheeled his bed over for a better look. "As for your father, once he's back on his feet, I'll show him around personally."

Buck leaned back with a grin that covered his entire face.

"I'm sure he can't wait," Paul said.

They were on the tram when Ava described the bunker's layout. "As you may have already discovered, portions of Sugarloaf Mountain were hollowed out to accommodate the bunker's four main facilities. Ark One is a ten-story structure which houses the living quarters along with the mess hall and entertainment area. Meals are served at 0900, 1200 and 1800 respectively. Forty-five minutes is the allotted time to eat. Miss your window and you don't eat."

Autumn crinkled her lip. "Ouch."

"The entertainment area contains a movie theatre with seating for three hundred. Nearby is a games room where residents can unwind playing pool, foosball, table tennis, cards, what have you."

"What's table tennis?" Paul asked.

Susan punched his shoulder. "Uh, ping-pong."

"I knew that."

The tram sped through the tunnel as Ava went on. "For those who are so inclined, the living quarters also house a fully equipped gym."

"It sounds more like a country club than a bunker," Paul observed.

"That's precisely why we don't use the term bunker," Ava replied. "A bunker's an ugly slab of concrete with dim corridors and tiny square rooms. The sort of place where Hitler spent his final days. The Ark is new, modern, spacious, perhaps the only one of its kind."

She seemed to be savoring the words the way a connoisseur might savor a vintage bottle of wine.

The tram slowed and then came to a gentle stop. The doors slid open with a hiss and the four stepped onto the platform marked Ark Two. Ava led them through a set of doors into what might have passed for the reception area of an office building. People here were mostly dressed in either white medical robes or orange coveralls. But all moved with a purpose, flashing identification cards at wall panels to open doors or pass through turnstiles. Two guards sat at a desk lined with monitors while another pair roamed the corridors, disappearing out of view. An elevator opened and took on a group of workers heading for God knew where.

"This is the science and engineering wing," Ava explained. "The upper floors of each Ark contain additional residences for those working in each area."

"Where do you stay?" Paul asked, resulting in an elbow from Susan. "I didn't mean it like that."

"I stay in Ark Three, the administration and COG department."

"So I guess the living quarters are sorta like steerage on the Titanic?"

Ava checked her watch, seeming to ignore the comment.

"COG?" Autumn wondered out loud.

"Continuity of government."

That was when the stark reality of the situation hit Paul. This wasn't a country club or some fancy vacation spot. This was the country's final and desperate attempt to hold itself together before it was ripped apart by anarchy.

Ava waved her hand in front of her. "Electricity from the Greers Ferry Dam nearby is sent via underground cables to Ark Two. If the outside supply is somehow cut off, deep reservoirs of diesel fuel will power a series of generators for a month or more. Ark Two is also responsible for sustaining life in other ways. Air from outside is drawn inside, purified and circulated throughout the main facilities."

"What about water?" Paul asked, suddenly becoming aware that his throat was parched.

"A massive aquifer beneath the mountain is our main source. Should that run dry, there are reservoirs available in addition to the ones dedicated to cooling the

31

generators. If push comes to shove, we always have Greers Ferry Lake."

"It sounds like this place has backup plans for the backup plans."

This time Ava did smile, sort of. "Is there any other way?"

Just then they heard a familiar voice behind them. They turned to find Brett, wearing green fatigues and looking bashful. "I was hoping I could steal Autumn away for a moment," he said. "Show her around a bit."

Paul opened his mouth to tell Brett, "Thank you very much, but she's already on a tour," when Susan cut him off.

"I think that's a fine idea, Brett. As long as you're okay with it, Autumn."

His daughter was beaming. Her cheeks, touched with the remains of a summer tan, now glowed a brighter shade of red.

The two of them left, leaving Paul concerned. "I don't think that's such a good idea," he half whispered to Susan.

"I knew what you were going to say and I think you need to relax a bit."

"Relax? We hardly know this boy."

Susan fixed him with one of those stares which usually signaled trouble. "That *boy* is the only reason we're alive right now. If it wasn't for him we'd probably be dead along the interstate from radiation poisoning. Besides, he's kind of cute and Autumn could use the distraction."

"That's what you thought about the last one and look what happened there."

He had a point and he could see it slowly registering in Susan's eyes. Chet had also seemed nice before Susan had been forced to plunge a knife into his back.

"This one's different," she protested. "I can feel it in my gut."

Paul folded his arms. Brett hadn't needed to lend them a hand, she was right about that. She was also right about him saving their lives. Paul swallowed hard, making an audible clicking sound. "Okay, but the first sign of trouble and I'm calling it off."

Susan smiled. "Your daughter's a stronger person than you sometimes give her credit for, Paul."

He winced. Perhaps she had a point there too.

Ark Three, the administrative area, was the next stop on their tour. This place was occupied almost entirely by military personnel along with government types in dark suits. Ava led them up a few floors and into an impressive command center. The focal point was a semicircular wall brimming with giant screens. Each displayed a map with a portion of the country. Many showed red blobs, which Ava told them represented nuclear fallout. Facing that wall were rows of desks with men and women in front of computers, wearing headsets. There was so much frantic action that it was difficult to catch more than a word or two from any one of them. As they were turning to leave, another tour group of wide-eyed civilians entered behind them. More and more this was starting to feel like a trip to Disney's Epcot Center.

"In a worst-case scenario," Ava told them once outside, "the remaining congressman and senators will take up residence here to continue running the country."

"But this place already seems kinda full," Paul noted. "I mean, there are over five hundred members of Congress with another four hundred in the Senate. Where would you put them all?"

She didn't answer, not at first, but Paul thought he already knew the answer to that. "But what about the rest of us in the living quarters?"

Ava looked grim. "You're right, the Ark is already operating at near full capacity. Let's just hope we never need to make those kinds of decisions."

By the time they reached the fourth and final area of the bunker, the heavy mood had been dispelled.

"Wow, so this is the Park we've heard so much about," Susan exclaimed as they exited the airlock.

All at once Paul was hit with a barrage of sensations. A cool breeze, the smell of pine trees and another sound he couldn't believe.

"Are those real birds I hear chirping?"

Ava nodded with pride.

The size of the place was more than impressive. If each of the other Arks formed a triangle, then the edges of the Park probably touched each of the tunnels connecting them. Paul glanced up at the ceiling only to shield his eyes from what looked like a glaring sun.

"How is this possible?"

"An LED projector that emits white light in a spectrum designed to mimic rays of sunlight," Ava explained. "In order to simulate Rayleigh scattering, we've added a thin coating of nanoparticles. It's easily the largest indoor biosphere on earth."

A small bridge led across a babbling brook and onto a gravel path. But there wasn't only a single path, there were several and they led in a number of different directions. All around was lush grass and every kind of deciduous tree you could imagine. Even more impressive was a large body of water with people in rowboats, enjoying a beautiful summer's day. The three of them crossed the bridge and followed the path, Paul marveling at the sights around him, big and small—the wind whispering through the leaves, the gravel crunching under his feet. He was in a dream, he was sure of it.

Susan pointed to a field where animals were playing in the grass. Paul wanted to rub his eyes. "Are those cats and dogs?" he asked in disbelief.

Ava nodded. "We have over fifty species in the Park. All of them specially bred to coexist in the Ark. We've... tempered their more aggressive genetic traits."

"In a moment, I just know Susan's gonna nudge me to stop snoring."

Susan giggled, sounding like the young woman he'd known years ago.

"When I told you the Ark was one of a kind, I wasn't exaggerating," Ava told them. "Like the real sun, the lights above will track across the sky, changing to shades of red, orange and yellow. In the evening, another set will illuminate to simulate stars. We knew how important it was for the human psyche to have reminders of the outside world. This is why the digital windows in your living space show scenes of the outdoors and why we included a park filled with the sights and sounds of nature."

Paul shook his head in amazement. "Cats and dogs getting along. If ever I needed proof that the world was ending, this was it."

"But this isn't the end," Ava told him. "Think of it as a new beginning." She smiled, this time for real.

If ever there was a Garden of Eden, Paul thought, this was it.

Chapter 7

Autumn was on the main floor of Ark One doing the last thing she would ever have expected. Before her, Brett slid across the smooth wooden floor, releasing the heavy bowling ball with the flick of his wrist and watching as it spun towards its target in lazy circles. His pose made Autumn giggle—right arm in the air, right leg behind him and pointed at an unusual angle. The shiny black ball roared forward, barreling into the stack of pins, knocking them all over.

"Strike!" He straightened, a beaming smile on his lips, his spiky blonde hair and handsome features accentuated by the warm glow of the lights overhead. He was still wearing his military uniform, which made him even more irresistible.

Brett tumbled into the seat beside her. "Guess that means I won the bet."

"What bet?"

He grinned. "You don't remember? If I won, you'd let me treat you to lunch. If you won, you'd let me treat you to lunch."

Autumn laughed. "I don't remember having that conversation."

"Early onset of Alzheimer's. You better look into that."

She slapped him playfully, becoming conscious of the grumbling in her belly.

"I hope you didn't hear that," she said, mortified.

Brett stared directly in her eyes. "Hear what?"

Not long after they made their way into a large mess hall. Rows of skylights overhead filled the room with artificial brilliance while circular tables filled an almost endless white room. Workers in coveralls moved past them, carting food supplies to be stored away. Seemed Autumn and the other refugees who had arrived weren't the only ones getting sorted. But this was less of a restaurant than it was a beautiful-looking cafeteria. From the pristine lunch line came the vague odor of meatloaf and spaghetti sauce. A few of the tables were already being occupied by residents waiting for lunch service to begin.

Brett took Autumn by the hand and led her up to the counter. He handed her a tray and grabbed one for himself. He was such a gentleman. This was the kind of thing she could get used to.

As they approached the serving line a woman began to tell them lunch wouldn't be for another ten minutes. Brett waved a white keycard with his picture on it. She nodded and asked them what they'd like to eat.

Autumn couldn't help but be impressed. He ordered the beef stew while she chose the lasagna.

"I like a girl with an appetite," Brett told her.

Seeing them with food, a man rose from a nearby table and approached the lunch line, only to be turned away.

"I play a lot of sports," she explained. "I'm not your typical salad-and-water type girl."

"I like it."

They sat and he asked about the sports she played and where she'd gone to school. She wanted so badly to tell him she'd played for the Panthers, but the truth was she'd never got an opportunity to try out, not before things went crazy.

As they ate, Brett continued to ask questions. He wanted to know everything about her. The sad truth was there wasn't a whole lot to say. She'd grown up in Nebraska. Her father owned a music store and her mother worked in real estate. Even with the pressure to make her life sound more exciting, she purposely didn't mention the rock band her father had once been a part of. It wasn't like Brett would know who The Wanderers were, nor did they have millions to show for it. Besides, no one wanted to be caught bragging over something that wasn't all that impressive.

Soon Autumn turned the conversation back to Brett. He explained he came from a long line of military men, dating all the way back to the Revolutionary War. Then the topic of Brett's father came up and his mood began to shift. In 2003, his dad had gone to Iraq and never come home. His eyes welled up with tears, but he fought them back.

"I was only six years old," he told her. "Young enough that I didn't understand why, but old enough to feel the heartache."

She reached out and touched his hand. It was trembling.

When the figure appeared, casting them both in shadow, Autumn immediately retracted her hand. He was an older man dressed in a dark suit—sixty, maybe seventy years old—with clouds of curly white hair in the back. His face was strangely shaped too, wide at the temples and tapering down to a thin, bony chin.

"Good afternoon, Brett," he said before turning in her direction. "And good afternoon to you, Miss Edwards. I trust you and your family have gotten settled all right."

She nodded, feeling uneasy but not knowing why. The man was grinning, yellow tar between his teeth from age or too many cigarettes.

"Excellent," he replied before the muscles in his face relaxed. He reached out and plucked a small flower from behind her ear. It was a magic trick and Autumn's heart started beating again. "We all need a little magic in our lives, don't we?" He handed her the violet. "Consider this a gift for a beautiful young woman."

Autumn took it and did her best to smile.

"I'm Director Van Buren," he said. "You may already be aware that I run this facility. If there's anything you need, anything at all, please don't hesitate to let me or my assistant Ms. Monroe know about it."

"I will," Autumn said, sheepishly.

Van Buren grinned and walked to another table where he introduced himself all over again.

"He seems nice," she lied.

"I shouldn't tell you this," Brett said, glancing around to make sure they weren't overheard. "But the director gave me crap after we arrived."

Autumn leaned forward. "Really? What for?"

"My commanding officer let him know I fought to have you and your family brought to the bunker. Said you weren't on the list."

Autumn's brow scrunched with confusion. "The list?"

"Of the chosen few, I guess. Isn't a big shock the rich wanna keep this place all to themselves. Van Buren's the head of some big military contracting company hired by the government. I'm pretty sure he was letting me know that inside the Ark, I answer to him."

"But shouldn't your commanding officer have been the one to speak with you?"

"Normally yes, but in here, all bets are off."

Chapter 8

Paul, Susan and Autumn were back in their single-room suite when they heard a rapid series of knocks at the door.

"You expecting someone?" Susan asked Autumn. Her gaze soon found Paul, who had returned from the men's communal bathroom at the end of the hall, his wet hair slicked back from a nice hot shower. A few more of those and he might begin to forget about being doused with ice water during the decontamination process.

"I'll bet anything it's Brett," Paul said, straightening his tunic.

Autumn threw him a sharp look. The knock came again, this time louder. "Well, if no one else is gonna answer it, I will." In three quick strides she was across the room, gripping the handle before flinging it open.

On the other side of the door was a man with a wild head of white hair, decked out in a tunic similar to theirs, several sizes larger. The grumpy look on his face left no doubt who it was.

"Grampa!" Autumn shouted, jumping into his arms. "You're better."

Buck rocked back on his heels, gripping the doorway with both hands. She was still hanging onto him as he entered swearing.

"The shoulder, honey," he squealed. "For the love of God, watch the shoulder."

She bounded to the ground, apologizing.

"Shouldn't you be in the infirmary?" Paul asked.

"With those masochists?" Buck shot back. "Always taking blood, sticking me with needles, not to mention my backside still hurts from that 'auto-injector'." He made air quotes as he said it. "Heck, I was starting to feel like a slab of meat. One more day and you'd have seen the last of ol' Buck, lemme tell you."

Paul laughed. "We could only be so lucky."

"But your IVs," Susan said.

"Tore 'em out."

"Dad, the doctor said you were dehydrated, that you needed liquids."

"Ain't you never heard of tap water?"

Susan crossed her arms.

"Don't be fooled, that wasn't no doctor. He's a quack with a wall full of fake degrees."

Paul hung the towel up laughing. "He isn't in the room five minutes and the conspiracy theories are already flying."

"Listen here, Rock Star, I'd like to see you in there, you wouldn't last five minutes."

"How did you find out what room we were in?" Susan asked, apparently abandoning all hope of talking sense into her father.

"I followed the stench," Buck said, grinning as his eyes settled on Paul. "No, I made 'em tell me. Same way I made 'em give me something to wear other than that Godawful robe. Would you believe even the smallest draft crawls right up your legs."

Paul went to the table and sat down. "I believe it. Has anyone shown you around?"

Buck's hand went to his hip. "Show me around? Are we at Disneyland or something?"

"I thought you were excited to see Ava again."

Buck's face soured. "I don't know where you're getting your information, but it's wrong. I gave myself a tour before I came and found you. Wanted to get my lay of the land and all that."

"So you saw Ark Two and Three?" Paul asked.

"What about the Park, Grampa? Tell me you saw the Park."

"Yeah, I saw it."

"And let me guess," Paul said. "You weren't impressed."

"Why should I be? It's a bunch of grass and trees and lovey-dovey animals."

Susan smiled. "He was impressed, he just doesn't want to admit it."

"What I did see were those radiation meters on the wall in every corridor. Judging by the readings things are getting a little too hairy out there right now, but as soon as they clear up, we'll make our way home."

"To what, Buck?" Paul wondered. "The tiny bunker under your barn?"

"Well, it's better than the non-existent bunker under yours."

"He's not knocking it," Susan cut in. "Paul's just wondering what the rush is to leave when we have more room and resources here."

"Maybe, but I don't like it."

Even Autumn was surprised. "Really, Grampa? It's actually quite beautiful. How can you not like this place?"

"The Ark itself isn't the problem," Paul said. "What Buck's trying to say is that he can't deal with authority."

"You never could," Susan observed, folding a towel in the bathroom and setting it back on the rack. "Least, not since you served in 'Nam."

Buck's face reddened. "I don't need to explain myself to you. All I know is as soon as the air outside is decent, I'm outta here, with or without the rest of you."

Chapter 9

The next morning, Paul made a decision. If they were going to be stuck in this bunker for the foreseeable future, then he would do his utmost to get back into shape. His first task was to find Craig and beg him for a pair of shorts, sneakers and a t-shirt. It took some time to find the man, and when he did the expression of confusion on Craig's face wasn't a complete surprise. From what Paul had seen so far, the military, scientific and political personnel in the complex had little time for luxuries like staying in shape. They were a busy bunch, securing the facility and organizing a response to the terrorists who had done this while trying to maintain at least a semblance of government. It was the busy bees wearing the science lab coats who puzzled him. Why were they always rushing about so frantically?

After a moment or two of begging, Craig finally caved in and finagled an extra pair of beige pants which he said could be cut into something resembling shorts. And who knew, Craig told him, maybe Paul would start a trend.

Ten minutes of hobbling pathetically around the track that circled the weight room and another ten struggling to bench a hundred and twenty pounds left Paul feeling like he'd actually accomplished something. Stealing a glance at the clock on the weight room wall, he saw breakfast was about to be served and headed for the mess hall.

The soft light spilling in from the artificial skylights was a surprisingly close approximation to morning. If he didn't know any better, he could almost convince himself he was standing in the center of a shopping mall food court. After a moment scanning the faces of those in the lunch line as well as friends or family members reserving seats at tables, Paul finally spotted Susan near the front of the line. He waved and hurried over.

"What on earth are you wearing?" she asked. Others around them were starting to stare.

"Shorts," Paul told her. "Stop judging. I went to work out this morning."

"You cut your only pair?"

He touched her shoulder. "I talked Craig into giving me a spare. I gotta say, I woke up this morning feeling good, but after pumping iron I feel fantastic."

The disturbed look on Susan's face wasn't going away. "I don't know who you are, but I want my husband back."

Paul laughed, grabbing a handful of extra meat on his right love handle. "Give me a month and all this stuff'll be gone. I'll look like an Adonis. You won't be able to keep your hands off of me."

He could see she was trying not to smile. The lunch line inched forward. "You've lost your mind." She grew serious. "Do you really think we'll need to be here that long?" she asked. There was an innocence to her question that touched Paul's heart.

"Honestly, I don't know. It could be less or it could be more. When Buck and I left Nebraska to come find you and Autumn, the only thing on our minds was keeping you both safe. What does it matter if that's here or in a cramped bunker buried under Buck's hay barn?" He caught her eye and saw something there. "You're not in as much of a hurry to leave either. I can see it. Don't forget I know you, honey," Paul said. "You're afraid that if you let down your guard this place'll grow on you and you might never want to go."

After they got breakfast—Paul a cup of fruit and a mineral water; Susan two eggs, bacon and hash browns—Paul and Susan found a seat.

"Did you know that next to the weights is a music room?" he told his wife.

She cut open her egg, sunny side up, and let the yolk slowly cover the bottom of her plate. "You must be happy."

"Happy? I'm thrilled. I saw a rack of acoustic guitars by the back wall. After breakfast I might swing by and exercise my fingers a little." He smiled and swirled his spoon before diving in and scooping out a melon ball.

Susan scanned the mess hall. The hum of conversation from the tables nearby was loud and he wondered why she was so preoccupied this morning.

"What is it, honey?"

He followed her gaze and spotted Buck, several tables over, engaged in a boisterous discussion, waving wildly.

"Oh, no," Paul said, letting his spoon fall into his fruit cup. "When Buck gets excited, bad things happen."

"He's talking to a group of men we haven't met before."

"Your father may not be the most agreeable man on the planet, but he's certainly no wallflower."

"Paul, go over there and sit with them."

"What?"

"Look, you know my father, he's probably trying to convince them the moon landings were faked."

Paul wasn't convinced, but she wore the pouty face that always got her way.

"You know his heart's in the right place," she said. "He's probably hurt because we didn't back him up yesterday."

"I'll go," Paul said, "but mainly because I'm sure those poor folks are too polite to admit he's driving them crazy."

Paul got up and headed over, past a young family of five and a table of men and women in military uniforms. As he drew nearer, Buck's voice grew louder and louder until there was no longer any doubt what he was talking about.

"If you thought we had a democracy before all this then you're a bigger fool than I took you for, Earl," Buck shouted. Across from him were four other men. The one he was calling Earl was a thin, middle-aged man with pleasant features. A patch of curly hair around his chin made him look like a billy goat.

"I ain't no fool," Earl said in a thick Arkansas accent.

"Maybe not," Buck replied. "But there's been a coup d'état. President's been usurped by a man named Perkins. He's already declared martial law in the big cities. Who knows what he'll do next."

"Who is this Perkins?" one of the other men at the table asked.

"I think he was a congressman?"

"What does it matter?" Buck said, bringing his fist down on the table. Some of the people around them were starting to look uncomfortable. Others got up and left. "The illusion of democracy is gone, gentlemen, that's the point I'm trying to make. We're living in a dictatorship. Unchecked executive powers. President Saddam Hussein."

"You don't know that," Paul said from behind him.

Buck turned, his cheeks blooming red. "I wondered when you were gonna show up. Tell them what that soldier said back in Atlanta. Go on, tell them."

Paul swallowed hard. "First of all, Edmund Perkins isn't a usurper. He was the Speaker of the House and next in line if anything should happen to the president and vice president."

"Yeah, ain't that convenient," Buck said.

"When we're stuck down here, it's hard for any of us to know what's true and what isn't," Paul told them. "Buck is telling the truth though. We did hear news that Perkins had assumed power in a coup. But if any of you have ever played the telephone game..."

"Telephone, smeliphone," Buck chimed in. "Whatever those terrorists were hoping to achieve they've done so much more. When we start throwing out the rule of law in order to fight back, then you might as well kiss the whole thing goodbye."

The folks seated around them weren't the only ones feeling uncomfortable. Paul didn't think this kind of talk—true or not—did anything to help the people who'd come here searching for a safe haven. Paul had faith that whoever the new president was, he would do everything in his power to uphold the Constitution and restore the rule of law. On that front he did agree with Buck. Without those two things, there was no longer a country worth fighting for.

49

Chapter 10

Later that afternoon, following a stint in the music room tuning guitars, Paul borrowed the Gibson acoustic and brought it to the Park. Getting there from Ark One wasn't all that difficult. Each of the three main facilities had their own access point—in this case, a pair of heavy steel doors led to a kind of airlock. The purpose was to maintain the Park's environmental conditions while also ensuring that none of the wildlife escaped.

A woman standing next to Paul in a white lab coat was holding a plastic container with a sandwich.

"Lunch break?" Paul asked, making polite conversation as a group shuffled into the airlock.

She nodded. "We don't get much time to eat, but I find the Park relaxing, so I try to make the most of it."

"I couldn't agree more." The strap holding the guitar to his back was over his shoulder and he gripped it with one hand to make sure it didn't hit someone.

The airlock quickly filled up. Lunchtime rush, Paul supposed. Soon, a red light became green and the forward hatch opened.

"I'm new here," Paul told her as they began moving out. Already he could hear birds chirping in the distance.

"Yes, I can see that."

He smiled. "I was given a tour the other day and I couldn't help but wonder." He paused, searching for the most diplomatic way of asking. "What exactly do you science folks do around here?"

Smiling, the woman looked up at him. She was shorter by about a foot with pale skin and tightly cropped black hair. "The trees, bushes, flowers and grass you see in the park," she said, motioning around her. "That's us."

"Oh, yes, that makes sense. You're a botanist."

"Some work in genetics, breeding the aggression out of some of the wilder beasts."

"I'm sure I know a human or two who could use some of that."

She smiled politely.

"I heard there was a jaguar in here somewhere," he said, kicking a stone off the gravel path.

Her face lit up. "There is. Her name is Inti, named after the Incan sun god, but I've only seen her once. She's magnificent. To answer your question, the bulk of my colleagues work in virology."

That last part took a second to sink in. "Virology? Doing what?"

"I'm not sure," she replied, tightening her grip on her sandwich container. "I guess you could say I don't have a 'need to know'. Maybe you should ask one of them yourself."

"Maybe I will," Paul said, holding out his hand and officially introducing himself.

"Victoria," she replied. "This is a good place, Paul. Don't ruin it by asking too many questions."

51

She walked away then, leaving Paul to ponder whether she was offering him a bit of friendly advice or a warning.

Not long after, Paul was strolling along, soaking in the artificial sunlight when he spotted a familiar face seated at a bench nearby. He swung his guitar around and began his best rendition of *Moon River*. Susan saw him coming and her face lit up with surprise and embarrassment. He loved teasing her and the playfulness of their relationship had kept them going through the rough patches any couple faced. As he drew closer, strumming and drawing hoots of encouragement from passersby, Paul noticed Susan wasn't alone. Nestled in her lap was a tabby cat.

When he was a few feet away, Paul dropped to one knee and ended with a grand finale. A small crowd had gathered around and they applauded. Susan shook her head.

"You're such a showoff," she chided him, as he set the guitar down and plopped into the seat next to her.

"That's why you love me."

Slowly the audience evaporated once they realized there wasn't going to be an encore.

"What's her name?" Paul asked, decidedly uncomfortable.

Susan dug out the cat's nametag. "Simba."

"Cute."

"You're allergic, I know," she said. "But it says here she's hypoallergenic."

Paul laughed. "I didn't know they were making cats the way they made pillows."

"Go on, pet her. See what you've been missing."

With some reluctance, Paul reached out and stroked the animal's back.

"Oh, come on, don't be a wuss. You don't pet a cat like it was a dog." She took his hand and used it to really

52

massage Simba's back. Purring, the animal rolled over and exposed her belly.

"See, she likes you."

And much to Paul's surprise, he liked her too. The sensation of running his fingers through the cat's orange coat was more pleasant than he'd imagined. There was something almost relaxing about it. Staring at her belly, Paul noticed something strange.

"You said this was a female."

"That's what the collar says. Why, were you going to ask her on a date?"

"It's just, I don't see any nipples."

Susan looked. "Yeah, you're right. That's weird."

"I met a woman in the airlock on the way in," Paul told her. "She worked in the science facility and said they had botanists and geneticists who'd made everything in the park."

"Made? It sounds so strange when you say it that way."

He nodded, pausing as he ran his fingers through the cat's fur. "I felt the same way. Growing life in a test tube just feels unnatural." He trailed off, deciding there was no sense telling her about the rest of his conversation with Victoria, least not before he could make sense of it for himself. "The rad levels got higher today," he said instead.

"That's the scariest part," she said. "If you were outside, you'd never know there was anything wrong. Radiation isn't something you can smell, taste or see. Not before your skin starts to bubble and your hair falls out." She was petting the cat faster now.

"It'll pass, honey. I promise, sooner or later it'll pass and we'll head back to Nebraska and everything will be okay." The lie rolled off his tongue with such ease, he was tempted to believe it himself.

It was frightening to consider just how much things had changed in such a short amount of time. And what about all those people who didn't have bunkers to hide away in? Would the drive home be littered with millions of the dead and dying? Nagasaki and Hiroshima were the only nuclear detonations over a major city and that had been decades ago, with weapons probably far less powerful. They were the lucky ones and Paul hoped his family, including Buck, remembered that.

"Have you seen Autumn?" he asked.

"She left first thing this morning, right after you."

"To do what?" Paul asked.

Susan scratched the top of Simba's head and the cat lifted her chin in appreciation. "I'm not certain, but I bet I could guess."

"Brett again, eh? Seems she's spending nearly every second she can with that young man. Doesn't he have a job to do?"

"That's what I told her. If a girl looks too desperate boys will lose interest."

That wasn't exactly where Paul was going. "I won't lie, I'm not exactly rooting for this love connection," he told her. "And I'm not sure either of us should be encouraging it."

"Why not?"

"Because she should be doing something more constructive with her time."

"Oh, come on, Paul, you're being a little too protective. You need to start trusting your daughter. She isn't a child anymore."

That was easy for Susan to say. Sometimes it wasn't easy for women to understand the protectiveness a father felt for his daughter. One never set out to win the Overbearing Father of the Year award. You tried to be cool, let them stumble and make their own mistakes, but when something bad happened you could spend a lifetime blaming yourself for not being there when they needed you.

Susan didn't need to plead her case any further. There was no doubt that Brett had done so much for them already, but a debt of gratitude didn't equate to carte blanche. Given what had happened with Chet, Paul would keep a close eye on things and make sure nothing got out of hand.

Those very thoughts were coursing through Paul's head when Craig approached Susan and him.

"Mr. Edwards."

Paul looked up, shielding his eyes from the glare of the artificial sun. His chest tightened painfully. "What is it, Craig?"

"Ms Monroe asked to speak with you right away. She said it was urgent."

Chapter 11

The woman at the reception desk in the Ark Three administrative complex looked about as friendly as a black mamba. Impossibly skinny, with narrow facial features and a permanent frown, she probably hadn't laughed in a decade or two.

The atrium of Ark Three was bright, with high ceilings. Men and women in suits were coming and going. It might have passed for the ground floor of a Manhattan skyscraper.

"I'm here to see Ava Monroe, my name is…"

"Yes, we know who you are, Mr. Edwards. She's expecting you. Top floor, first office on your right."

A bank of elevators were behind her and Paul began heading in that direction.

"Not so fast, Mr. Edwards." She handed him a pin which read 'visitor'. "PFC Sanchez will escort you up."

A soldier with tightly cropped dark hair stepped forward. "Shall we?"

The receptionist buzzed them through a turnstile. Once in the elevator, Sanchez used a white keycard to unlock the control panel. Paul's stomach churned as they shot into the air. He couldn't shake the sensation he was being sent to the principal's office.

The whole way here he had run through what he might have done wrong. He'd been on the tram when he'd finally figured it out. They'd discovered one of the guitars was missing from the music room and figured out he'd been the one who took it. A high-tech place like the Ark surely had cameras all over the place.

The elevator doors swished open and Sanchez motioned him forward. Ava's office door was open. The décor was simple enough. A desk, computer and two chairs. It was more what was missing that struck him. Plants, pictures of family or beloved pets, the sort of things most people kept close at hand.

"Thank you," she told the soldier who stood by the entrance. "Close the door behind you." Her voice sounded cold and a touch dismissive and Paul couldn't help but notice how that frigid demeanor tempered her stunning good looks.

"Grab a seat, please, Mr. Edwards." She indicated a chair on the other side of the desk.

Paul did as he was told. "You can call me Paul."

She smiled weakly.

"Am I in trouble or something? I mean, I didn't see a sign-out sheet for the guitar. It needed a little tuning up and I had every intention of bringing it back when I was done." He was babbling and the confusion on her face told him it was best to shut up and let her do the talking.

"This isn't about a guitar," she told him. "This is regarding a disturbing event which occurred in the mess hall."

"I don't follow."

"Your father-in-law—his name is Buck, I believe."

"Yeah, what about him?"

She leaned forward and laced her fingers together. Her nails were short and devoid of polish, and Paul didn't notice a ring. Not that he was looking for one.

"He was heard spreading false information and frightening several of the other residents."

"The rumors of a coup," Paul said, the pieces clicking into place.

"Yes, that's exactly what they are, dangerous rumors and he needs to stop. I shouldn't have to explain to you how grave the country's predicament is at the moment."

"No, trust me, you don't."

"You may see them as harmless, but that kind of talk is a poison. A single careless comment could easily distort the delicate equilibrium inside the Ark, Mr. Edwards…"

"Paul," he interrupted.

"A poison that eats away at the morale," she went on without taking a breath. "Losing that is akin to pulling a thread on a sweater. Before long the whole thing begins to unravel."

"And Buck's right to free speech?"

She smiled condescendingly. "We want Buck to exercise his better judgment, just as you've chosen to exercise your physique."

Paul's eyes went wide. "How on earth did you know about that?"

"Craig told us about your conversation earlier and we commend you for keeping yourself busy in a responsible fashion. That's the point I'm trying to make. Buck has time on his hands and you know what they say about idle hands."

"Yeah, they're the devil's workshop."

A grin formed on Ava's glossy lips. "That's right."

58

"But why are you telling me this? Shouldn't Buck be the one in the hot seat?"

"I'm appealing to cooler heads," she replied. "Buck is more likely to listen to a family member when it comes to matters like this."

"You don't know Buck."

Her face grew serious. "And you don't know us. I'm sure I don't need to remind you that your wife, your daughter and father-in-law are all here as our guests."

"We're United States citizens," he protested.

"A cute line from the movies we've heard often lately. You are citizens and as such your responsibility is to maintain the collective peace. If that means a bit of self-censorship and common sense, then so be it. I would hate to be forced to eject you all from the facility. As you know, the conditions outside are getting worse by the day. Without the proper protection, the cells in your body would begin to break down almost at once. Radiation poisoning is a horrible way to go, let me assure you." She grinned again, opened a drawer and produced a piece of cake. "Do you like cheesecake, Mr. Edwards?"

"Uh, no, thanks. I just lost my appetite."

The last thing he saw was her look of disappointment as he walked out, making sure to close the door behind him.

Chapter 12

Still in the COG bunker on the outskirts of Washington, President Edmund Perkins entered the cramped office, closed the door and took a deep breath. His body felt weak and his throat was killing him. In the last several days, he'd been in meeting after meeting, trying to pull the country away from the brink. It wasn't a surprise that everyone wanted a piece of him. The Joint Chiefs of Staff, the heads of the FBI, CIA, NSA, DHS... the acronyms went on and on and on.

He'd expected the loss of life to be dramatic, but he hadn't anticipated the toll it would take on him. In the days after the attack, sleep had evaded him. Whenever he closed his eyes, millions of dead Americans were staring back at him, their expressions filled with condemnation. He was a male version of Lady Macbeth, his hands soaked with blood he couldn't wash away.

But they sure as hell hadn't died in vain. That was a mantra he'd taken to repeating whenever the thumping headaches became too much. Not unlike soldiers in past wars, these heroes had given up their lives to help forge a better America. A stronger America. It didn't matter that the recent dead hadn't volunteered or even known a battle was coming.

Perkins settled into the plush leather chair and lifted the receiver of the red encrypted phone on his desk. The line led straight to the Department of Defense. A soft female voice answered.

"Please authenticate."

"President Edmund Perkins."

"Analyzing, please hold."

Perkins waited, tapping a pen against the desk.

Then another woman's voice came on the line. "Yes, Mr. President?"

"Get me a line to the Ark."

"Right away, sir."

A click and then a quick series of rings, the way phones rang in London and parts of Europe. A man answered.

"I was wondering when you would call." It was Van Buren and he sounded cross.

"It's a lot worse than we thought," Perkins explained. "I'm at my wits' end here."

"Toughen up, you're the leader of the free world now."

"The DHS is estimating five million dead already with plenty more to follow."

"That's a start at least. Have you ever tended a garden, Edmund?"

"No, I can't say that I have."

Van Buren let out a hollow laugh. "You had people who did that for you, didn't you?"

Perkins didn't answer.

"Sometimes to save a plant you need to trim some leaves. You're doing the right thing. Do not despair."

He sounded so sure of himself. Perkins wished his faith was as strong. If the old man only knew the half of it. The true nature of their relationship.

"Listen, Edmund, there's something I need to talk to you about. Rumors of a coup have started trickling through the complex. Talk that the president's been overthrown."

The breath caught in Perkins' throat. "I don't see how that's possible. Those Secret Service men assured me they would use the utmost discretion."

"Well, they didn't," Van Buren barked. "And now I'm sitting in a bunker beneath a million tons of rock, reading reports about riffraff agitating an already precarious situation. Part of our strategy involved a seamless transition of power. That's why we made you Speaker of the House, remember?"

"I'll have those Secret Service men taken care of," Perkins suggested, stumbling over his words.

"Don't bother. The damage is done. How soon can you get here?"

"I need another few days."

"You have seventy-two hours. After that, phase two of Project Genesis will begin."

Chapter 13

It was fascinating the way a mess hall took on the dignified auspices of a grand dining room simply because a different meal was being served. Sure, the lights were dimmed and candles placed on each of the tables, but otherwise there was no real difference. One was still required to line up clutching a plastic tray like they had all those years in high school.

Without a doubt, the military personnel as well as Ark employees seemed a little cleaner and more comfortable, some even wearing casual clothes like jeans and t-shirts. Civilians, on the other hand, didn't have that option anymore since their clothes had been torn from their backs and incinerated during processing. All civvies were dressed in the same dull earth-toned tunics and loose-fitting pants.

On a lighter note, it did seem that Craig's prophecy about Paul's new shorts starting a trend was coming true.

As early as mid-morning, Paul had noticed more than a few slacks cropped at the knee. Most of them, he guessed, were unaware that Paul had only mangled his reserve pair. Either way, the trend was catching on and the sight offered Susan and him a nice moment of levity.

Unlike breakfast and lunch, which were governed by the first-come, first-serve rule, dinnertime was a different beast altogether. This was Paul's second such experience and each time the rules changed. Day one had seen a single sitting, which had quickly become a disaster since everyone showed up at once. On day two there were two sittings, one at 1800 and another at 1845. On day three there were three sittings, the last marked for 1930. The warm lighting and candles were a nice touch.

Susan and Buck had gone early in the morning to reserve a table for the first sitting only to discover yet another change had been made. Civilians were to eat at one end of the room while military and Ark personnel ate at the other. A distinct class system was beginning to emerge and its appearance did nothing to settle Paul's nerves, still frayed after his conversation with Ava earlier in the day. She'd threatened to have Paul and his family—Buck included—ejected from the bunker and left to die in the cloud of radiation sweeping over them at this very moment. The digital rad readouts dotting every other wall made it clear that the levels outside regularly exceeded six thousand mSv, well within the zone of lethality.

Since the meeting, Paul had struggled with whether or not to tell his wife about the rather unveiled threat Ava had delivered—keep Buck quiet or else. Paul knew he'd have an easier time convincing the Columbia River to flow in the opposite direction than he would telling Buck to watch what he said. And when he'd attempted to protest on constitutional grounds, Ava had practically laughed in his face. He'd been under the mistaken impression that free speech, even during a national disaster, was a right worth fighting for. But to what authority would he appeal to enforce his inalienable rights? If the director's assistant would have none of it, then how could he expect to find a sympathetic ear with Van Buren himself?

As they shuffled through the growing dinnertime crowd to their designated table, the anxiety in Paul's gut became downright painful. With every step it was becoming increasingly clear what he must do. Pull Buck aside after dinner and try to talk some sense into him. If the crotchety old bugger could be made to see the bigger picture, they might all get through this in one piece.

The first sign Paul's plan was destined to blow up in his face reared its ugly head the minute they took their seats. The tables sat ten apiece. Paul, Susan, Autumn and Buck settled in, followed quickly by Earl Mullins, his wife Cindy and their two children, little Earl Junior and Colton, a little boy with a prosthetic left arm. The last to join were the two men Paul had seen Buck arguing with earlier, Jeb Wilks and Allan Womack.

It turned out Earl, a mechanic from Heber Springs, had received a visit from the National Guard shortly after the nukes went off and had been told the fabric of society was about to break down and that a spot inside a local government facility was awaiting them.

Jeb and Allan had similar stories, except each of them lived nearly a hundred miles apart. And like Earl, they were both working-class folks from rural areas. Where their stories parted was at their marital status. Both Jeb and Allan were single and childless. That wasn't to say the two men didn't have family somewhere, but with military men standing in their faces and no one sharing their homes, they both said they'd made a quick decision, and one they were starting to regret.

"I was sure the folks in the big cities would be hit worst by the chaos," Jeb told them. He was squat with an impressive belly and a neck the same width as his head.

Allan nodded. Thinly built with pronounced veins running along his forearms, he looked like the calmest of the three. "I told those army types I was gonna stay, but they tossed me into a truck. Told me they were saving my life. Left my two dogs behind with no one to feed 'em." His eyes welled up with tears and he blinked them away.

"They may have used kid gloves in my case," Earl said. "But practically the first thing they done was remove my AR-15 along with both pistols I'd stashed in a bag. Waited till we were halfway there before doing it too. Didn't leave us any choice but to comply. Wasn't like we could just up and walk home. Now we're stuck wearing these damn prison rags. Saw a handful of folks this afternoon who'd even cut their damn pants into shorts, like they were on holiday or something."

Paul felt a hot flush rise up his neck and into his cheeks.

"Idiots, I tell you," Jeb threw in.

Buck was seated next to Paul and his eyes fell to his son-in-law's bare legs. Buck shook his head in disgust before adding his two cents. "With us, they waited till we were here before springing their little trap. I was unconscious at the time with a gunshot wound, but let me assure you if I'd been up, no one woulda taken my guns." Buck was leaning forward now, his own protruding belly pressed against the edge of the table. In usual style, Buck was taking a shot at Paul for not arguing to bring his guns inside the bunker. It was only a question of time before he laid the entire terrorist attack at Paul's feet.

"I think the line's dying down," Paul cut in, trying to defuse the escalating tension. "Maybe we should get some food."

"Any of you notice something different about the dining room tonight?" Buck asked the group.

"Come on, Buck," Paul pleaded. "Don't do this."

"I'll do what I damn please." He looked at the others seated there. Even with Buck's raised voice, Earl didn't seem worried his wife or children might be upset. In fact, they were hanging on Buck's every word.

"Well, the lights are a touch more romantic," Jeb offered.

Autumn smiled. "The candles are a nice touch."

"I'm not talking about the candles. Look around you. We're sitting in a sea of puke beiges and barf browns, while the upper classes have a section all their own. Mark my words, it won't be long before civilians are forced to eat during the last sitting, if at all."

"They have to feed us," Paul protested.

"Do they? These people have already taken our clothes, our guns, our dignity. It's bad enough we've suffered a devastating attack by a bunch of savages who hate the freedom we stand for. And then to top it off our rights and liberties are stripped away one at a time. I wonder what Emperor Perkins will have to say about this."

Paul snapped and shouted before he could stop himself. "Stop it, Buck, or you'll get us thrown out."

People around them had stopped eating and were staring, some with open mouths, tonight's dinner on full display. Not far away, Van Buren leaned against a pillar, arms crossed, watching the spectacle for himself.

"Thrown out for speaking my mind?" The look of disbelief on Buck's face surprised even Paul. "You're quick to toss away your rights and freedoms and for what? So you can live another day. Is that all it takes, the promise of a warm meal and a roof over your head? Regardless of what you might have heard, this is still the United States of America. I'm not gonna give up on my constitutional rights just yet and I hope the rest of you won't either."

The crowd erupted in applause and Buck stood there, just as surprised by their reaction. Earl rose to his feet and whistled loudly.

When Paul looked back, Van Buren was gone and along with him any hope of talking some sense into Buck.

In the old days of sail, a seaman's greatest fear—apart from fire—was that a cannon would come loose in heavy seas and smash through the hull, sinking the ship. That was the reason they were lashed with heavy rope. It was also the origin of the term 'loose cannon'. As Paul had come to discover, the Ark was a kind of ship and Buck the cannon threatening to tear from its berth and send them beneath the waves. Ava had ordered Paul to use those heavy ropes to silence his outspoken father-in-law and he had failed.

And yet as frustrated as Paul was with that failure and Buck's stubbornness, he also recognized the truth in what the old coot was saying. Deciding between a set of sacred principles and the lives of your family wasn't easy. Paul had hoped in entering the bunker, he would be shielded not only from the radiation, but from the requirement to make those kinds of life-and-death decisions. Not only had he been wrong, fate had a rather sick sense of humor.

Chapter 14

Not long after, Paul was back in their sleeping quarters staring out the window, or at least the digital image of a pasture with rolling hills and dairy cows that passed for one. There was something rather disturbing about it since the chances were good a scene like this would look far different today. Sure, the grass in the field might still be green, but the livestock would be little more than bloated corpses dotting the landscape. Even the predators were likely dead. An entire cycle of life upended. Part of Paul wanted to know just how bad things were out there and another part didn't think he could face a reality that bleak.

Susan entered the room a moment later.

"Well, it seems Buck's found himself a new fan club."

Paul didn't answer.

"Look," she said, sitting down next to him. "I know you were trying to talk some sense into my father, but you've gotta face the fact that your 'voice of reason' approach simply pushes him further to one extreme."

Paul heard the words Susan was saying. He just couldn't bring himself to tell her the truth.

"He's no spring chicken, Paul. Folks get set in their ways and the chances are good he won't have some miraculous change of heart. Maybe it's time you accept him for who he is."

At last, Paul turned. "Does your father drive me up the wall? Trust me when I say that's putting it mildly. Like your new friend Simba, sometimes I wonder if he was genetically engineered—to push my buttons."

Diane rubbed his back. "Believe me, I know. I'm often left wondering who's the married couple here, us or the two of you."

Paul couldn't help but grin. "He's too hairy for me."

They both burst into a fit of laughter, Paul doubling over until the hot tears came streaming down his cheeks. Susan covered her mouth with both hands and quivered. She was self-conscious of her teeth, which was silly because they were beautiful, but those little vulnerabilities made him love her even more.

When they finished, the muscles in Paul's belly felt like he'd just finished ripping through a hundred crunches. Laughter was part of Mother Nature's exercise regime. Sometimes letting off steam was the only thing that stood between you and insanity. As he pulled Susan into a hug, his hand running through her fiery red hair, he decided to break his word.

"Buck has a big mouth," he began and she pulled away and gave him a face. "I know I'm not telling you anything you don't already know," Paul said. "Much to my own surprise, I learned the hard way there are moments when that big mouth and belligerent attitude can come in handy. If it wasn't for him, we probably wouldn't have made it to Atlanta in the first place."

She smiled. "He said the same thing about you."

That hit Paul like a load of bricks. "Really?"

"Don't be so surprised. He may not show it, but he thinks more highly of you now. Probably wasn't more than a day or two ago that he and I spoke and he said there were a few scrapes where your diplomacy and calm manner saved the day. Even admitted if he'd been alone, his mouth would have landed him in a heap of trouble."

Paul laughed. "I must be dreaming."

"You've gotta understand, Paul, that kind of talk is so hard for Buck. He'd rather swallow molten lead than let himself be vulnerable, especially to you."

"I get it, I suppose. We've got some kind of sibling rivalry thing going on."

Susan shook her head. "No, you're wrong. He sees you as a son, Paul. The one he never had."

"Well, I wish he had the strength to tell me that himself. How odd that he isn't afraid to knock someone's head in, or give them a piece of his mind, but when it comes to showing any kind of tender emotion, the guy just crumbles."

"Are you any better?" Susan asked and her words hit him with the force of a left hook.

He hated when she made so much sense.

She touched his back before getting up and starting to walk away.

"I never told you about my meeting with Ava," Paul began when she was halfway across the room.

She turned. "I thought you said nothing happened."

His eyes went back to the digital window and the cows before returning to his wife. "I did and I lied. I was trying to protect you."

"Protect us from what?" Her arms were crossed now, as though she were getting ready to block a blow. "You don't think I've noticed how beautiful she is?"

Paul sat upright with a start. "What? Oh, for God's sake, no. You know I had some wild times back in the eighties touring with The Wanderers, but believe me, those days are ancient history. Susan, you're the only one for me. Besides, hasn't Buck already lined her up in his sights?"

She smiled weakly. "He'd kill you, you know."

"I don't doubt it."

"Forget it, I guess I was just having a moment."

"Well, we've got bigger worries."

"What did she tell you?"

He drew in a deep breath and held it. "You remember the other day in the mess hall when Buck was shooting off his mouth?"

"Yeah," she replied, the word drawn out.

"Someone must have reported him to the administration because Ava called me in and insisted I shut him up."

"Shut him up? What about his right to free speech?"

"Trust me, I said all that, but she went on about how dangerous rumors could be and that if he didn't stop they'd throw us out of the bunker."

Her pale, freckled hand clamped over her mouth. "Oh, no, Paul."

"Believe me, honey. You're the last one I wanted to burden with this. I've been fighting back and forth since that meeting, but after what happened at dinner, I just don't know what to do."

"I still don't fully understand why they're trying so hard to shut him up."

"She said it was a morale issue, that talk of the coup d'état and the government coming undone was dangerous."

Susan nodded. "I guess I can see that, but to threaten to kill people? 'Cause that's exactly what it would mean, Paul. Make no mistake about it."

"Don't you think I know that? I see those radiation readouts glowing red all day long. It's all I've been thinking about." He pointed to the digital window and the cow pasture almost as proof.

"Then we simply need to come clean and tell him," Susan said.

"Really?" Paul wasn't at all convinced. "Don't you think that'll just be putting a match to gasoline?"

"Probably, but what other option do we have?"

She fell into the computer chair and shook her head. "Can they really do that, Paul? It's surely against the law."

The sardonic laugh came blurting out before he could stifle it back. "What's to stop them? There aren't any cops or courts we can appeal to. We're at their mercy."

"We should never have come here," Susan said. She was up and pacing back and forth now.

"If we hadn't we'd probably be glowing with radioactivity. We were between a rock and a hard place and we made the only decision that made sense. Choosing death is never a viable option."

Susan stopped and raised her index finger to her lips, a move which puzzled Paul. Was something passing outside in the hallway?

She approached and whispered into his ear. "What if the room is bugged?"

"Okay, now you're starting to sound like Buck. Of course the room isn't bugged. There's nothing worth listening to, Susan, and I'm sure those suits in Ark Three have better things to do with their time. The entire fabric of our country's on the brink of unraveling."

Susan paused before her gaze rose and caught his. "What if they're the ones responsible?"

Chapter 15

Susan's words were still ringing in Paul's ears the following day when Paul asked Buck to join him in the park after breakfast. With a, "Sure, why not," Buck had agreed and followed him for a bite to eat. But even the early-morning crowds gathered in the mess hall, shuffling for seats in their designated areas, couldn't shake that strange feeling he had.

The very thought that even a faction of the US government had had anything to do with the terrorist attack was too egregious an accusation to take seriously. Susan had thrown it out there the way most of us tend to with wild theories without contemplating the larger implications. Although he hadn't admitted it at the time, the idea that the rooms were bugged had stuck with him and was the reason why Paul had wanted to speak with Buck in the Park. At least there, nature might provide the sort of privacy they needed.

Not long after they finished eating, Paul and Buck excused themselves and set off for the airlock which led from Ark One into the Park.

"I heard a rumor they might be adding snakes," Paul said, trying to make polite conversation.

Buck grunted. "I hate snakes."

"These ones will be genetically modified."

"Yeah? Well, look where our GMO food got us. Ain't never a good idea to muck with nature."

So much for polite conversation, Paul thought as they entered the airlock. It wasn't as full as the other day even though there were still quite a few people. On their way out of the airlock, another group entered on their way back to Ark One.

In the middle of the green space was a large artificial pond and that was where Paul and Buck were headed.

Along the way, they crossed paths with a man pushing a woman in a wheelchair. Paul had seen them around from time to time during these first few days, noticing they mostly kept to themselves. From what he'd gathered from Susan, they were a young couple, the wife suffering tragically from osteogenesis imperfecta, a disease which made her bones so brittle, a single pat on the back could crush her spine. The illness had reached the point where she could no longer walk and was wheelchair-bound. Paul waved as they passed, the man waving back.

"Hell of a life," Buck commented before they were out of earshot.

"Geez, you could at least wait till they can't hear you."

Buck laughed. "You PC types kill me. You don't mind one bit making snide remarks behind someone's back, but God forbid they should hear you."

"I just don't see the point in hurting her feelings."

"But you were thinking the same thing I was, weren't you?"

Paul wanted to lie, but didn't. "Maybe I was. A degenerative disease like that is worse than a death sentence."

"Lemme tell you, they wouldn't get much further than a diagnosis before old Buck took matters into his own hands."

There Buck went, talking in the third person again. "There may be a life lesson in that sort of thing."

"Yeah, the lesson is, better off dead."

They stopped along the edge of the water. The artificial sun was still low in the sky. Around them, other civilians were milling about. A few of them stretched out beneath the maple trees. Others rowed on small boats across the pond, smiling or giggling at one another. Buck reached down, scooped up a handful of stones and began tossing them in one at a time. The water made a bloop sound as each one went in.

"You know, it's a crazy thing to think about given what's going on out there," Paul said. "But people here really seem to be enjoying themselves."

Another stone and another bloop.

"It's 'cause they've let the wool be pulled over their eyes."

"They should be unhappy?"

"I'm not sure about unhappy, but definitely not nearly so darn complacent. See, that's the problem with folks. You give 'em comfort and a little distraction and they're more than happy to hand over every last ounce of their personal responsibility. Safety slaves."

Paul kicked a small rock into the water and grinned. "Safety slaves. I've never heard that before."

"Course you haven't. I just made it up. But it's the truth. You take care of people's basic needs and they stop asking questions. Grumbling bellies are the first sounds you hear in any revolution. I ain't saying anything crazy. In the real old days, the Romans spent a ton of money on gladiatorial games to distract the mobs of Rome from rising up. Before all this," Buck said, waving his hand in a wide arc, "we were pacified with movies, sports and above all else, television. Heck, they didn't call it the boob tube for nothing."

"Sounds like the urban legend about department stores piping subliminal messages over the PA."

"Yeah, now you're getting it. 'Don't steal.' 'Buy more worthless stuff.'"

The two men laughed.

Buck tossed a fresh stone. "By the way, if Earl Mullins comes up to you, don't give him the time of day."

Paul's eyebrows rose. "I thought Earl was a friend of yours. He gave you a standing ovation after your speech in the dining hall."

"That's what I thought, before I discovered the guy ain't nothing but a two-faced punk."

"He was talking behind your back?" Now Paul was genuinely interested.

"Nah, I passed him in the corridor this morning. He was with his family and he gave me the cold shoulder. You know me, Paul. I don't take kindly to being snubbed, so I raised my voice and even pulled his arm. Hey, maybe he went deaf in his sleep last night. Anyway, he stared at me like I was a stranger and herded his family away like I was the big bad wolf. Won't be surprised if those other two do the same."

"Jeb and Allan?"

"Haven't seen them since. I ain't got no use for people who turn on you at the drop of a hat."

Paul's mind was turning a mile a minute. "Maybe he became uncomfortable with all the conspiracy talk."

"No way, Rock Star. Earl was more of a hardcore conspiracy theorist than I am. Every time we got to talking he always found a way of bringing the conversation back to 9/11. 'What happened to building seven, Buck?' he'd shout. 'What happened to building seven?' Like how the heck should I know?"

"But all that nonsense about a coup. The president being overthrown by a usurper."

Buck turned to him. "I was only repeating the same thing we both heard from Brett."

"He's a kid in a uniform," Paul replied. "What the heck does he know? And what if he's wrong, Buck? What's the payoff for getting everyone all riled up for nothing? It distorts the delicate equilibrium in here."

Buck stepped back and frowned. "Who got to you?"

Paul straightened. "What do you mean?"

"'Delicate equilibrium.' That doesn't sound like you. Sounds like someone gave you an earful and you're passing it along."

"No one spoke to me, Buck," Paul lied, wondering if someone had also given Earl a similar threat of being kicked out. He hated to fib, but revealing the truth would only strengthen Buck's outlandish idea that the director was aiming to enslave them. "You're being paranoid. All I'm saying is that it's best not to rock the boat too much before we know the score."

Buck grew quiet after that and the two men walked on for a while in silence. Finally they reached the airlock which led to Ark Two, the science and engineering complex.

"Let me show you what I mean," Buck said and headed through the airlock's heavy doors. A handful of others were inside with them, waiting for the red light to turn green. When it did, they exited into what might have passed for the main entrance of a pharmaceutical laboratory. Men and women were coming and going, some in lab coats, others in coveralls.

"Yes, I've been here, Buck. Ava brought us on a tour."

Buck kept walking.

"Hey, where are we going?"

"Stop whining and walk like you own the place," Buck growled.

The security men at the front desk were busy redirecting a lost civilian when Buck and Paul slipped past them. They rounded the corner and came to a bank of elevators. One of them was about to close when Buck stuck his hand in.

They climbed in, surrounded by science and engineering types who didn't hide their questioning looks.

Paul stared down at the control panel and saw there were ten floors above them and six beneath. Basement one and two both said engineering, but it was the classification of the other four basement floors which made the blood in his veins run cold. They were marked biohazard one through biohazard four in descending order. Paul clicked the button for biohazard one.

"I'm not sure you two are supposed to be here." A balding man in a lab coat spoke up from the back.

Buck cleared his throat. "We're part of a study on venereal diseases." He nudged Paul, who began scratching himself.

The balding scientist took a step back.

Two engineers got on right as the elevator began to close. The doors nearly touched when a bell rang and the doors swung open. Standing outside the carriage was the guard from the front desk.

"Come with me," he said.

Paul's heart sank. He'd been trying with everything he had to rein Buck in and all he'd managed to do was get himself into more trouble.

"Don't worry," Buck said. "Just let me do the talking."

Chapter 16

Paul and Buck were held alone in a tiny room for close to an hour. At last, two men in dark suits entered and sat across from them. They were armed, their pistols swinging back and forth from the shoulder holsters they were wearing. The trick, Paul knew, would be to play dumb and act dumber.

Which was why Paul spoke up before Buck had a chance to open his big mouth. "Listen, gentlemen, my father here is old and senile," he told them.

"What are you talking about?" Buck shouted, but the bone-white hair on top of his head wasn't doing him any favors.

Paul gave them a pained look and half whispered. "Denial. It ain't just a river in Egypt, let me tell you."

They smiled weakly.

"You gentlemen were in a restricted area," one of the agents said.

"See, here's the thing," Paul told them. "Pa loves to ride the elevator. Up and down all day long. It's like a religion for him. Only thing that keeps him from pulling his hair out. A side effect of all the medication he's on. Anyway, we were walking through the park and he started yelling, 'Upsy downsies,' which is his way of asking for an elevator ride. You can't imagine how unbearable he gets when he doesn't get his way—"

One of the security guards poked his head in.

"Agent Vickers, phone call for you. It's the director."

Paul's pulse quickened.

Vickers rose and left the room.

"Is there anything else you want to add?" the other agent asked.

"Yeah," Buck replied. "Something in this place stinks."

Buck wasn't making this easy and Paul had to think fast. "Oh, Pa, that's just your colostomy bag come undone again."

Buck looked at him with eyes that promised a swift beating when this was over and done with.

Vickers came back into the room and stood by the door. "You two are free to go."

"We are?" Paul said, trying and failing to hide his surprise.

"Please head back to Ark One immediately."

"You'll never see us again," Paul promised.

They rose and filed out.

Both agents watched as they walked through the reception area and headed toward the tram. A stroll through the park would take too long, and besides, Paul's legs were still weak.

"You nearly got us killed back there," he scolded Buck after they'd reached the platform. A digital display indicated the next train was due in five minutes.

"Nonsense. Our taxes paid for this place. We had every right to see what's going on."

"I think the men with the guns might disagree."

At the far end of the platform, Paul spotted the two agents, watching them.

"Are they really wearing sunglasses? That's so cliché."

"You suppose they're trying to intimidate us?"

"Not more than they already have. I'll bet they're here to make sure we go back where we belong."

Buck glared at them.

A moment later, the tram roared into the station. Paul and Buck got on and took a seat. Slowly, the train pulled away for the short journey to Ark One.

"I'm still trying to work out what all that biohazard stuff was for."

Paul considered this for a moment. "Your guess is as good as mine."

"Saw a documentary on lethal diseases. Stuff capable of wiping out the human race. We're talking biblical plagues here."

"Yeah, I get it," Paul said, wringing his hands.

"Those bad boys are normally given a biohazard level of four, the same level we saw back there."

"Maybe they're working on vaccines," Paul offered. "We've seen how these bunkers are designed to protect and maintain important branches of the government. Well, maybe this is where the CDC is now headquartered."

Buck nodded. "That does make sense."

"And if you're right about the danger of a level four biohazard, then it begins to make sense why they wouldn't want unauthorized people snooping around. Might also be why they gave us an inoculation when we first arrived."

Buck spat. "My rear end still smarts."

Paul grinned, recalling the panic on the old man's face when he'd seen an inoculation was coming.

"Mine too," he replied, rubbing the spot where the auto-injector had done its damage.

Buck had raised some important questions. Paul could see the old man wasn't completely sold on his explanation. There seemed to be more than a few secrets floating around this place. A bunker dug into a hollowed-out mountain, top-secret areas shrouded in mystery, and more creature comforts than most of the civilians were used to.

It was then that it dawned on him. Something about the living quarters that Ava had told him during their initial tour. That they were initially designed to house members from the House and the Senate. At the moment the government and science people stayed in Arks Two and Three.

In that light, the stark reality of this installation began to come into sharp focus and it explained why they'd struggled so much in the beginning with the influx of civilians. This bunker hadn't been built with them in mind at all. In the event of a SHTF-type scenario, American civilians were considered expendable.

Chapter 17

The message over the loudspeaker came early the next morning.

"All residents from Ark One are required to present themselves to the science and engineering wing by 0800 hours."

Paul's eyes snapped open as the message blared again. It seemed to be on a loop. In the bunk above him, Buck snored away merrily, sounding like a wildebeest searching for a mate. Susan and Autumn were already up.

His daughter was worried. "What's going on, Dad?"

"I haven't the foggiest idea," he told her. "Last thing I remember I was dreaming about The Wanderers. We were set to go on stage and I couldn't find my guitar."

"You normally have that dream when you're stressed," Susan said, seated before the desktop computer. A tickertape along the top and bottom of the screen was repeating the message as it played over the speaker. Even the digital window was doing the same.

Annoying alarm aside, Paul was starting to feel the pressure of keeping Buck under control. Of course he hadn't told Susan what had happened in the elevator the day before. Wasn't any sense worrying her for nothing. Although Paul couldn't help but wonder himself if this assembly was somehow connected.

"How long before we need to be there?" he asked, feeling the overwhelming need to brush his teeth.

"Twenty minutes," Susan told him.

Paul looked up at Buck, the mattress on the upper bunk sagging under his weight.

"That should be just enough time to get Buck on his feet."

They reached the science and engineering wing twenty-five minutes later. Turned out waking Buck from a bad dream was just as deadly as waking a sleepwalker. Paul rubbed the bump on his forehead where Buck's knuckle had caught him square on the noggin.

"Coulda been worse," the old man said, looking rather satisfied with himself. "A few inches down and I'd have given you a real shiner."

Paul shook his head, eyeing the crowd already gathered. While most had opted to wait for the tram, others had chosen to cut through the Park. For the two men, this was something of a déjà vu since it had only been a few hours earlier they'd nearly been imprisoned on these very grounds by Secret Service types.

There must have been several hundred civilians gathered in Ark Two's Atrium, all of them dressed in the same drab potato-sack outfits. At least, that was what

Autumn had taken to calling them. All she'd talked about on the way over was Brett and what a sweetheart he was for trying his best to get her a better outfit. Paul's attempts to remind her she wasn't away at summer camp had been swiftly shot down by Susan. Since when did fathers no longer have a say in who their daughters dated?

An improvised platform and podium blocked off the narrow approach to the elevators. The crowd was filled with nervous energy. A million rumors were buzzing through the crowd. "They're throwing us out," some said. "They've run out of food and they're kicking us to the curb." Others joined in, offering a historical basis to back up the possibility. Castles under siege during the Middle Ages, they argued, often ejected the peasants and townsfolk as soon as the stores of food and water got low. Additional theories came, each more outlandish than the last.

"They got these people exactly where they want 'em," Buck said.

"Frightened?" Paul replied, not entirely sure he believed it.

"Don't you see? These sheeple have already jumped to the worst possible scenario."

"So?"

Buck gave him the look which said, *Stop being such a dullard.* "So, anything they propose now will seem like a huge improvement over banishment and death."

Just then Ava climbed up to the podium. She tapped the mic and it made a hollow sound.

"Isn't she great?" Buck said. "She's a natural."

"Yeah, a natural microphone-tapper. Susan, I think your father's having an aneurysm."

"Boys," his wife said in a motherly tone. "Be nice."

"Tell him that," Paul protested.

Buck shushed him. "I'm trying to listen."

"First and foremost," Ava began, "I'd like to thank you all for assembling this early. My apologies for our methodology, but we didn't know a less intrusive way of getting all nine hundred and fifty of you here on time."

Heads in the crowd looked around, as if to see what nearly a thousand people standing in one room looked like.

"In a moment, I'll be bringing Director Van Buren on stage to address you. Some of you have already been introduced, others have seen him around. But I'd like to take a moment to tell you a little bit about the man. Mr. Victor Van Buren came from humble origins. His parents both survived the Nazi camps and dreamed of a fresh start in America after the war. Starting out as a shoeshine boy, Mr. Van Buren quickly demonstrated a knack for business the *New York Times* said was unparalleled since the likes of Cornelius Vanderbilt. In a few short years, he transformed a humble shoeshine business into a veritable empire. Always in search of a challenge, in the 1980s he bought a little biotech company named Novogen and grew it into one of the largest Fortune 500 companies in the world. With architecture, construction and bioengineering firms, Mr. Van Buren was an easy choice to build the next generation in protective installations. The Ark was a facility we hoped we would never need, but America's enemies made sure we did. The country outside the protective confines of these walls has been hurt, horribly wounded, but not fatally. Not by a long shot. The dust will settle as it did after 9/11, as it did after Pearl Harbor, and when it does we'll leave here together knowing within each of us is the key to rebuilding a better, stronger America. Please join me in welcoming the man to whom we owe a tremendous debt of gratitude, your director, Mr. Victor Van Buren."

87

The reception area exploded with thunderous applause and it only increased as Van Buren stepped onto the stage. Tall and dressed in a dark grey suit, he reached the podium and adjusted the microphone.

"It won't be easy following up that wonderful introduction," he said, nodding to Ava Monroe.

A smattering of laughter from the crowd.

"Our great country will rise again one day," he began. "This isn't a political slogan. I'm speaking from the bottom of my heart. I'm also speaking as a man with a plan, as the kids like to say these days, because the first step in America's rise begins with a brand-new initiative: Work for Food."

Paul and Buck exchanged an uneasy look.

"Each and every one of us needs to pitch in and do our part. This nation achieved greatness on the shoulders of generations of hard-working Americans and I plan on calling on that strength today. There are jobs for everyone here in the Ark and the rules of the program are simple; the work you do will be paid in vouchers which you can exchange for food and drink."

Murmurs passed through the crowd. People might have hated the circumstances that had brought them here, but they'd certainly grown accustomed to a leisurely existence. As Buck had mentioned earlier, many lived their day-to-day existence as though they were on vacation. The lack of newscasts showing the devastation and desperation outside only helped to cement the illusion. And now the director was telling them all that was about to change. They would be expected to earn their keep and worse, failure to work would result in a failure to eat. He hadn't exactly come right out and threatened to have them ejected, but many probably sensed it was not far off.

"What about those who can't work?" a woman near the front row shouted. "I'm fifty-nine and on disability."

A man close by joined the growing chorus. "My wife is wheelchair-bound with brittle bone disease. Will she be expected to work?"

Van Buren seemed to be prepared for this reaction. "Those with legitimate claims can make an appeal to be excluded. Remember, not every job need be strenuous. Even routing incoming calls or filing documents can be helpful. I will, however, offer a warning. Anyone of sound body or mind falsely claiming disability will be subject to the harshest penalty."

He never came right out and said the word 'banishment,' but the implications were clear enough.

Van Buren grinned. "You look like a terrific group of people, you really do. I'm certain it won't come to that." Ava came and whispered something into his ear. "Oh, yes, I nearly forgot. The forms you see being passed through the crowd are to be filled out by anyone fourteen years and older. Remember to list any applicable skills, no matter how insignificant they may seem. Tables with clerks are being set up on your way out to collect the documents."

Buck received one and read it aloud with derision.

"'Do you have any experience in the construction field?' 'Have you ever worked in a hospital?'"

Then Paul received a stack, and passed one to Susan and Autumn before handing them to a man behind him. "'Have you served in the military?'" He looked over at Buck. "That's a yes for you."

"Here's what I think of Van Buren's work program." Buck held the questionnaire about a foot from his chest and tore it in two and proceeded to tear the remainder into smaller and smaller pieces.

"Dad, are you crazy?" Susan scolded him.

"Those Nazi camps Van Buren seems to wear as a badge of honor used to have a sign that hung over the front gate with a message prisoners would see upon entering. It read, 'Work will set you free,' and it was just as much a lie as this program is. They don't need the help. They need to keep us busy, keep us from snooping around. And I suggest each of you tear your sheet up too." Buck snatched the one from Paul's hand and tore it in two.

Paul yelped as though he'd been shot. He turned to the man behind him, but the stack had long since moved on.

"You're gonna get us killed," Paul snapped.

"I'm freeing you."

Paul looked at Susan and Autumn, who had already gotten a pen.

"Let me borrow your back so I can fill this out," Susan said, and somehow the words stung. "Don't worry, you can get one on the way out."

Not long after, they began pushing through the crowd toward the exit. Just as Van Buren had said, tables were manned by clerks collecting the forms. What he hadn't told them about was the presence of soldiers behind them.

"If this isn't a police state, I don't know what is," Buck spat.

But there was more than one stop before they'd be allowed to leave. Standing between the clerks and the soldiers were men in white lab coats holding auto-injectors.

Buck's eyes went wide and Paul could tell he was thinking about that first painful injection they'd received.

"This way," Autumn said, pulling them along. She pointed at one of the soldiers they recognized as Brett.

Susan and Autumn handed one of the clerks their papers and passed through to get a shot.

"What is it?" Paul asked the clerk, who looked on coldly.

"A vaccine against cholera. It has a nasty habit of breaking out when this many people live in such close proximity." He searched Paul's empty hands. "Your papers?"

"I didn't get one."

The clerk's face dropped. "You can't leave before you fill one out."

Autumn and Susan were waving them on, but Paul could only shrug. A moment later, Brett showed up and whispered something in the clerk's ear.

The clerk looked back at Paul and Buck. "All right, go ahead."

They had no sooner passed through than a squat, mean-looking nurse pressed an injector against Paul's arm and pulled the trigger. A blast of air was followed by a sharp pain. Buck was next and his face went white as the short nurse approached him. For the old man, the only thing more frightening than getting a shot was having it administered by someone so small.

"Grow a pair," Paul shouted, watching Buck's face contort with fear.

After that, they headed back to Ark One. Upon arriving, lines were already beginning to form in the mess hall for breakfast. Today would be the last time to grab a free meal and it seemed no one wanted to miss out.

"They'll start imposing limits," Buck predicted. His eyes found Susan. "You saw firsthand in Atlanta how people descended on grocery stores like a pack of wild animals. Mess with a man's food and you bring out the beast."

Autumn touched Paul's arm. "Brett said they'd be posting guards to protect the kitchens during meals and after hours as well."

"There's been a shift," Paul noted. "It wasn't so apparent before, but now it's become unmistakable."

"A shift in power?" Susan asked him.

Paul shook his head. "No. A shift in policy. They don't feel the need to keep us bloated on pleasant distractions anymore. Win us over playing Mr. Nice Guy."

Buck couldn't agree more. "From here on in, it'll only get worse."

Chapter 18

Brett's apparently noble attempt to get Paul and Buck scratched off the workforce didn't pan out as well as expected. Far from excluding them, their failure to hand in the proper documents earmarked them for a special, even distasteful, job.

The news came the following morning with an abrupt knock on the door of their room. Craig was the messenger and he informed them that they needed to report to the engineering section for garbage collection and disposal duties. While Paul had attempted to maintain his composure, Buck had flown into a tirade, belting out a greatest hits of curse words, many invented by the old man on the spot.

Thankfully, word from Craig hadn't nearly been as harsh for the girls. Susan and Autumn were asked to report to the infirmary. Susan, with her limited medical experience—the first six months of a failed nursing degree—would assist doctors in prepping and administering future inoculations. For her part, Autumn would join her mother as a nurse's aide.

Either one of those would've suited Paul just fine and he understood right away they weren't simply being punished for failing to fill in the form. They had been singled out for sticking their nose where it didn't belong.

Choosing to accept their fate, the two men made their way to the engineering wing without so much as a coffee or muffin for breakfast. True to Buck's prediction, dozens if not hundreds had tried the day before to sneak extra dinner rolls, pieces of fruit and in some cases saltine crackers. In nearly every case, soldiers stationed by the lunch line exits had been there to search them as they left. Those caught pocketing extra food were simply given a warning, but it was clear the penalties would become far more severe as time went on.

The two arrived about fifteen minutes later and found a man in dark blue coveralls, with short hair and a handsome face, waiting to greet them. Wearing an orange hard hat and a frown, this guy was all business and no pleasure right from the start. After two failed attempts at a joke, Paul had to admit Chief Engineer Richard Hardy had about the same sense of humor as a nest of wasps.

He handed each of them a pair of bright yellow coveralls, yellow gloves and a matching hard hat.

"I heard the two of you are trouble, so I'm gonna make this real simple," Hardy told them. He sounded like a New Yorker. "The darker the coveralls, the higher the rank. Sorta like karate belts, except we don't do white. Work hard and do as you're told and you'll be paid, maybe even promoted. Mouth off or break the rules and you'll discover all the different ways I can make your lives a living hell. We understand each other?"

Paul nodded while Buck glared in defiance.

Afterward, he brought them to a room where they changed. Initially Paul had simply pulled the yellow coveralls over his brown slacks and beige tunic until Buck had let him know he was making a terrible mistake.

"You ever work with garbage before, Rock Star?"

"I'm happy to say that I haven't."

Buck laughed. "You artsy-fartsy types kill me. Well, let me put it to you this way. You got one set of clothes in here and you're wearing 'em. You keep those on and I guarantee by the end of your shift you'll smell worse than a donkey's behind."

"So what do you recommend, oh garbage guru?"

Buck grinned. "I suggest we don't wear a thing underneath these coveralls and stash our clothes in one of those." He pointed to a wall of small metal lockers. Paul followed Buck's suggestion and dropped his pants.

"What the heck are you doing?"

"What? You said we should get undressed."

"Yeah, in the bathroom. Not right in front of me." Buck was shaking his head in disgust.

"Get over it," Paul shot back. "You're about to see a lot worse than this."

Once dressed, the two men stood facing one another.

"I feel like a giant chicken," Paul said.

"You look like one," Buck offered.

"If I hadn't let you rip that paper of mine, I could've been teaching a music class or something useful instead of getting stuck on garbage patrol."

"That's funny. This place needs a music teacher about as much as they need another litter of nippleless cats."

"Well, you never know."

Buck's face didn't show an ounce of doubt. "Trust me, I know."

Trying to hide their embarrassment, they returned to the spot where they'd met Chief Engineer Hardy and found a handful of men and women in yellow coveralls already gathered. Hardy was busy giving them his 'no-nonsense' speech.

On the far side of the atrium, government types in suits were chatting and laughing.

"Get a load of that." Buck pointed.

Paul looked, wondering which of Buck's arbitrary rules they had broken.

"Seems mighty hard to swallow getting called to task by the dictator, I mean director, when those bureaucrats are living the easy life." Underneath his bushy white beard, Buck's cheeks were turning red with anger. "First they burned our clothes and forced us to dress like a bunch of Hungarian peasants. Now they're sending us to clean up garbage while they live the high life. If they wanna class war, I'm more than happy to give them one."

Chief Engineer Hardy appeared next to them and shoved a mop into their hands.

"You were wrong, Buck," Paul said, eyeing the wooden pole in his hands as though it was a foreign object. "Apparently we aren't only garbage collectors, we're janitors too."

Buck groaned. "This keeps getting better."

Chapter 19

The rest of that morning and afternoon they spent performing a humiliating list of cleanup duties— mopping the atriums in Arks One, Two and Three, emptying trash cans into large plastic bins set to be incinerated. Lucky for them, another group of maintenance workers in yellow coveralls took the garbage to be burned, but the responsibilities around here were on strict rotation and it would only be a question of time before that particularly nasty job fell to them.

By one p.m., Paul was staring to walk funny. Not simply on account of the growing tightness in his lower back. His feet were throbbing with pain. That was the last place he had expected to hurt. Funny how we took our bodies for granted, barely aware of muscle and bone until one or both began crying out in agony.

In spite of the physical discomfort, Paul felt he was dealing fairly well with the situation. Sure, he hated being conscripted into probably the worst job the complex had to offer, but he kept reminding himself how it sure beat the alternative: starvation or, better yet, exile.

Buck, on the other hand, was managing his new role with about as much grace as a spoiled child. But unlike Paul, it hadn't been the manual labor that got to him. The old guy took pride in his physical prowess and his ability to work with his hands. He had built most of the barn in back of his property as well as the bunker beneath it all on his own. No, Buck's sore spot right now was his pride and he made no bones about expressing his displeasure.

Dumping a trash can into one of the large plastic bins, Buck whacked it against the side of the container with a loud boom. "You may not mind being a prisoner in this glorified excuse for a bunker, but I'm gonna tell you something, Paul. I've just about had it." He tossed the trash can back in place. It skittered across the floor and slammed against the wall. Paul went over and set it back in its place.

Paul returned to the other side of the wide corridor, where he was doing the same thing. "I'm no more a fan of this than you are, but stop being such a baby about it."

Buck ignored him. "Saw Jeb during that fifteen-minute excuse for a lunch break they give us. He's been put on maintenance too. Noticing a pattern yet, Paul? Speak out against the tyranny and they send you off to do hard labor." Buck pushed the bin a few feet and stopped to empty another trash bin. This one was by a set of bathrooms. Out came the can, boom, boom, boom against the side of the bin, then a grunt from Buck. Something was apparently stuck at the bottom. He reached in and pulled it out and convulsed with a fit of disgust when he saw it was a woman's used sanitary napkin.

"Oh, for goodness' sake."

Paul grabbed his belly with laughter. Living with two women, he was no longer shocked by such things. "I think you may have found your calling, Buck."

The old man threw him a look. "So Jeb mentioned that Earl Mullins and his family left last night."

Still on the other side of the hallway, Paul stopped what he was doing. "Really?"

The grin on Buck's face stretched from ear to ear. "Who knows, maybe he refused to work. Gave 'em the finger. Either way you slice it, Earl musta figured he was better off taking his chances on the outside."

Paul wasn't sure why the old man was smiling. Sure, Buck hated authority of any kind, but for Earl to risk his family's safety like that seemed reckless, maybe even criminal. The last rad meter he'd seen had shown levels still clearly in the red. Given that, their departure was hardly cause for celebration.

Perhaps seeing the objection on Paul's face, Buck said, "You can't stomp on a man's rights and expect him to sit back and take it."

"Well, you're arguing from principle, but Earl just doomed his wife and kids."

"I had a feeling you'd say that. Sometimes a principle is worth dying for."

Paul gave that one a moment to sink in. "I suppose that shows you were wrong about one thing."

Buck's eyebrow perked up. "Really? And what's that?"

"If Earl and his family were allowed to leave, then this place isn't a prison at all."

Buck didn't like that one and went back to his trash collection.

Not long after, they moved to the second floor of the administrative building. A meeting had been underway between the few members of Congress who'd made it to the complex. Since the Ark's blast doors had sealed shut behind them five days ago, not a soul had arrived and only Earl and his family had left.

Paul and Buck had been instructed by Chief Engineer Hardy to wait outside for the meeting to end. Once everyone left, they would clean up.

Far from a heated exchange, Paul was shocked by what they heard going on behind those closed doors. Lots of old men cackling over poorly told dirty jokes. Soon after the doors swung open and a wave of political types and their assistants came streaming out. A young man in a sharp suit emerged brandishing a paper coffee cup and an obnoxious laugh. He was sidling up to a grey-haired guy who must have been a congressman. As they passed, the kid held out his coffee cup for Buck to take. Buck's eyes narrowed as the kid let the cup go. It hit the ground with a hollow pop, coffee splashing over the feet of all three men. The procession stopped.

"What are you, some kind of an idiot?" the kid asked, surveying the damage. "I was handing you my cup and now you made a mess."

A sort of calm came over Buck. "No, you made a mess. You're a big boy, can't you throw out your own trash?"

"Excuse me?"

The congressman stepped in to prevent the situation from escalating.

Buck stuck out a hand and pushed him away. "Let your son fight his own battles. He's got a mouth on him, writing checks I'm sure his diapered backside can't cash."

Some of the congressmen chuckled.

The young assistant was half Buck's size, but his face was three times as red. Winding up, the kid swung a wild fist at Buck, who raised one of his giant forearms to block it.

"Thank you," Buck said and with that the blood drained from the assistant's face. One of Buck's giant paws clamped around his tie while the other curled into a fist and struck with the speed of a coiled serpent.

Buck's first punch made the assistant's knees give out. He drooped, Buck holding him up by the tie.

Like the early heavyweight boxer Jack Johnson, Buck didn't want this to be over too soon. The next blow landed into the mouthy assistant's gut, knocking the wind out of him and satisfaction bloomed on Buck's face as the arrogant twenty-something crumpled to his feet. It would only be later that Buck would complain about the pain where Finch's bullet had punched a hole below his collar bone during their struggle in Atlanta.

Predictably, the hallway erupted into chaos, but what they hadn't counted on were the two Secret Service agents who jumped on both of them, slapping Buck and Paul in handcuffs.

Chapter 20

That defiant look was still on Buck's face when both men were marched into the director's office. Dark and velvety, the room was spacious and filled with antiques. Van Buren was apparently something of a collector. On the wall were old paintings, many of them from the old masters. Paul wasn't quite educated enough to know them by name, but several he'd seen gracing the pages of many a coffee-table book. In one corner stood the armor of a twelfth-century knight. Not the full plate stuff you saw in museums. This was a suit of chain mail. The frayed white robe draped over it was emblazoned with a faded red cross.

"Once belonged to Sir Achard of Montmerle," Van Buren said from behind them. He was standing in the doorway, leaning casually against the frame. "He defended Jerusalem before it was taken back by Saladin in 1187. He'd sworn an oath to protect pilgrims traveling through the Holy Land from the west."

He entered, followed closely by Ava Monroe. She was wearing a pair of horn-rimmed glasses and Buck's face changed right away.

"Your girlfriend's here," Paul said.

"Shut yer mouth," Buck snapped.

"I see the two of you have a difficult time getting along with others," Van Buren told them as he circled around his desk. "We had a similar problem with another resident here…" He paused.

"Earl Mullins," Ava offered, filling in the blank.

"Yes, Mullins. I provided him with options, but he chose to leave. Accused me of keeping them here against their will. But I assure you that isn't true. The military personnel here at the compound hate to open those big doors unless they really need to, but I never want to be thought of as a warden."

"You people are treating us regular folks like peasants," Buck told him. "I think you forget who you're really working for."

Van Buren's lips curled into a smug little grin and even Paul wanted to punch him. "Have we?"

Buck's hands clenched into fists. "Treating us like second-class citizens, forcing us to work for food."

"How's that any different from your everyday life?" Van Buren asked. "I suspect it isn't. Do you not need to work in order to live? Does your government not already treat you with derision?"

It was clear Buck wasn't going to win this argument.

"We know about the labs in the basement, Franz," Buck said, struggling against his handcuffs. "I think we'd all like to know what killer bugs you're studying down there."

Van Buren's momentary surprise turned to wry laughter. "Believe me, we have nothing to hide. If you haven't already figured it out, the Ark is a repository for all the world's knowledge." He scanned the room. "This facility was built in the wake of 9/11 after the powers that be worried a catastrophic event could threaten our entire way of life. You may have noticed convoys of vehicles on your way here. Many of them were packed with rare treasures. But of course, I'm not only talking about gold and silver. I'm speaking about irreplaceable works of art and literature. I'm talking about a seed vault large enough to rival the Svalbard in Norway, not to mention digital copies of every book, movie and government report ever created."

Paul's jaw came unhinged. "You people don't think things are gonna get better, do you? You think the country is doomed."

"That's a bunch of bull," Buck shouted. It didn't seem to matter anymore that the beautiful Ava was in his presence. "You said yourself, Van Buren, we'll rebound. Unless you were telling lies."

"Oh, I wasn't lying, William."

He was using Buck's first name, Paul realized, but how did he even know it?

"America will rise again. The real question is: what will the country look like when it does?"

Van Buren waved a hand at Ava, who went behind Paul and undid his handcuffs. She then did the same for Buck. "It's a real shame to see you mixed up in this mess," Buck told her. "You're a beautiful woman, you can have any man you want."

Ava circled around, both sets of cuffs dangling from her index finger. "Who says I need a man?"

Buck's voice deepened. "I'd say you're wound up tighter than an eight-day clock. But that's nothing a good massage couldn't help alleviate."

Paul was starting to feel uncomfortable. Ava was younger than Buck's daughter, Susan.

Van Buren had apparently also heard enough. "What you've been told today was in the strictest of confidence. I trust you gentlemen will keep it between us."

"You mean keep our mouths shut that this place and the people in it represent the last remnants of a country we knew and loved? Those poor folks out there deserve to know they're locked in some sorta wacky social experiment."

"This is no experiment," Van Buren assured them. "When we emerge from here, we're all going to find a very different place than we left. That is beyond question. But spreading rumors of coups d'état and biomed facilities will only serve to create discord."

Buck shook his head. "Make the civilians harder to control, is what you mean, Franz. Let's speak plain English and quit beating around the bush."

Van Buren lowered himself into a plush leather chair. "I was told you had a stubborn streak and I believed it, but this is no longer stubbornness we're seeing. This is folly."

Buck perked up. He didn't seem to mind being called pig-headed, but he drew the line at being called a fool. "Pardon me?"

"A man concerned with his own preservation and the welfare of the ones he loves knows when to fall in line and do as he's told."

Paul couldn't help but laugh. "You don't know Buck."

Buck threw him a scowl.

Paul's hands flew in the air. "I'm just saying."

"Well, you ain't helping the situation."

Van Buren's eyes moved from the computer monitor back to Paul. "Mr. Edwards, I see here you own an instrument store up in Nebraska."

Paul's throat tightened. "Yeah," he squeaked. "I did before all this happened. Probably isn't much of it left by now."

"And you were once part of a musical group called The Wanderers." Van Buren grinned. "Even played on *David Letterman* in eighty-nine, is that right?"

"Only once and it was toward the end of our career."

Clicking the mouse again, Van Buren said: "I have no use for television. Rots the mind."

Paul nodded. "It can, some shows more than others. I guess what I don't get is how you know all this."

Van Buren's gaze returned to the screen. "I see your daughter was enrolled at Georgia State. Did she ever make the Panthers?"

Now Paul's discomfort rose a notch. "No, the terrorist attacks put an end to that…"

"And they said the NSA wasn't tapping people's phones." Buck groaned.

"Oh, William, we know a great many things, you're right about that." Van Buren made another click and appeared to be reading something. "For instance, we know of your military service in Vietnam."

The muscles in Buck's jaw flexed.

"Where's all this going?" Paul asked. He looked at Buck and something in the old man's face told him he knew perfectly well.

"We also know that on August fifteenth, nineteen sixty-nine you were dishonorably discharged."

Now it was Paul's turn to be surprised. "Dishonorably discharged?"

"It's a long story," Buck snapped.

Van Buren was enjoying this. "Oh, I'm happy to get into the gory details if it'll help."

Buck stood rooted in place, his face looking more and more like a freshly picked beet. Finally he said, "That's ancient history. Ain't no sense dredging up the past."

"I couldn't agree more," Van Buren said. He was standing now, his hands clasped in front of him. "I'm hoping we have an understanding then?"

106

Buck's eyes fell to the floor, leaving Paul to wonder what the heck had just happened. Never in all the time he'd known Buck had he seen the old guy shut down so thoroughly. What had happened in Vietnam all those years back was still a mystery, but Van Buren had made it perfectly clear that if Buck wouldn't keep quiet, then neither would he—a threat which had achieved everything it was intended to.

Paul convinced himself that by the end of this, when they were finally allowed to leave the Ark, far from any resentment, they would feel a tremendous debt of gratitude for Van Buren. He might not win any popularity contests, but when the chips were down, he'd taken them in, kept them safe and given them another chance.

Paul couldn't have been further from the truth.

Chapter 21

Susan had spent most of her first day at the infirmary, trying to swallow a sizeable dollop of guilt over the cushy jobs she and Autumn had managed to land while Buck and her husband had been conscripted into garbage disposal and floor-mopping. It didn't help ease that heavy feeling in her heart that Dr. Redgrave, whom she was working with, was a terrifically handsome man with a great bedside manner. Never mind what her crabby father had said about him being a quack. Buck couldn't spot a fake ID, let alone a forged diploma from Georgia State.

She and Autumn, along with eighteen other women of varying ages, had been commissioned as nurses. The truth was they were mostly nurses' assistants since very few of them had any real experience in the medical field. Which meant that the three women who had once worked in hospitals were expected to do some serious on-the-job training.

After getting a complete tour of the place, Susan quickly realized calling it an infirmary simply didn't do it justice. It was closer to an emergency room with several areas reserved for treating patients. Upon arrival, senior nurses would provide triage for newcomers to determine the level of attention they required. The categories were straightforward. Priority One meant anyone with a life-threatening case. Priority Two was for patients with serious issues without the immediate threat of death. Mostly lacerations, severe pain, high fever. Priority Three catered to those who needed minimal care. Small lacerations, sore throats.

Which led to the second area the newcomers were responsible for. Prepping for inoculations. It had been less than twenty-four hours since they'd received the last one. As Dr. Redgrave explained, these were preventative measures designed to reduce the spread of potentially deadly diseases. The bunker was something of an incubator. With so many people running around in a confined space, it was inevitable that sicknesses spread. All you needed to do was look at the outbreaks so common on cruise ships. The danger was all too real and the doctor's dedication gave her a feeling of comfort and reassurance.

The small glass vials with the vaccines needed to be kept cool and came packed in blue coolers, not unlike the kind one might take to the beach on a warm summer day. The procedure was simple enough. Whatever vials weren't used were sent back to the medical labs Dr. Redgrave told them were several floors beneath their feet.

Susan found Autumn in one of the minor procedure rooms, cleaning a child's bloody knee and applying a bandage. She smiled with pride at the delicate care her daughter was giving. One of the senior nurses named Wendy appeared behind her. She was packing up unused vaccines before carting them back to the labs and needed a hand.

Always willing to help, Susan followed her to a smaller room. In one corner a table was stacked with blue coolers and against the far wall stood a row of waist-high refrigerators. Inside the fridges were dozens, perhaps hundreds of vials. Without delay both women began carefully emptying them into the coolers. Before long, the back-and-forth repetition became second nature and Susan slid into a groove. It was only as she was filling the final cooler with vials that she actually read one of the labels. The writing on the tiny glass bottle was hard to read at first. Then, as the letters came into sharp focus, Susan was left scratching her head.

"What's Project Genesis: Phase Two?" she asked innocently. "And why underneath that does it say 'placebo?'"

Wendy certainly wasn't new here. She was one of the senior nurses and had been there to help inoculate Buck when they first arrived. She clearly had more experience here than many of the others. So if anyone should know what was going on, it was her.

Wendy had her hands elbow deep in one of the coolers. With a puff of air, the senior nurse blew the bangs out of her eyes and glanced up, looking decidedly uncomfortable.

"It's nothing. Don't worry about it."

Susan continued scanning the label, all manner of internal alarms going off at once. "I suppose I'm mostly wondering why it says 'placebo?' What exactly is in these vaccines?"

Without saying a word, Wendy straightened her back and glanced over her shoulder at the open door. "I really don't feel comfortable talking about this," she said.

Susan walked past her and pushed the door closed. "How about now, Wendy?" Her eyes fell to Wendy's hands and she saw that they were trembling. The sight sent a bolt of fear shooting up Susan's spine. She took the senior nurse's hands into her own. "Don't worry, whatever it is, you can tell me."

After taking a deep breath, Wendy spoke. "All I know is about two weeks ago, coolers filled with these vials began showing up."

"Before the attacks?"

Wendy nodded. "I asked Dr. Redgrave about them and all he said was they'd come from the bio labs on the lower levels."

"Bio labs?"

Wendy explained.

"Van Buren did own a biomed company," Susan said, putting some of the pieces together.

"Listen, I can get in a lot of trouble talking to you about this. Before arriving here, we were all made to sign strict non-disclosure agreements."

Susan closed the lid on one of the coolers and crossed her arms. "Maybe, but we're talking about people's lives here. This isn't only a legal issue, it's a moral one."

Wendy nodded. "Believe me, I take my job very seriously. I didn't sign up to hurt people, but these shots they're giving are only saline solution. We don't even inject it into the bloodstream. It's perfectly harmless."

None of this was making any sense. "Maybe it is," Susan said. "But what's the point of it all? Are they just trying to keep people busy? Or in line?"

"Those are questions I don't have answers to," Wendy told her and Susan believed she was telling the truth. "But I might know someone who does."

"I'm listening."

"First you need to be aware that for all intents and purposes you aren't in the United States anymore."

Susan took a step back. "What do you mean, not in the United States?"

"We're locked up inside a mountain, Susan. There aren't any courts in here to enforce any outside laws. And in case it hasn't already become abundantly clear, there's only one judge, jury and executioner in the Ark."

"The director?" Susan asked in a hushed voice.

Wendy squeezed her hands in affirmation.

"I appreciate the word of warning, but I still want the name of that contact."

"Dennis Dresselhaus. He's the supervisor for biohazard level one." Wendy closed the last of the coolers and began putting them onto a trolley. "Bring these to him and say that I sent you."

Susan's lips curled into a humorless smile. The Ark was starting to feel like an onion, wrapped in dark layers she was about to start peeling back.

Chapter 22

The walk from the infirmary to the elevator bank in Ark Two couldn't have been more than a hundred feet, but for Susan every step of the journey was taking monumental effort. She wasn't the kind of woman who liked to stir up trouble. She was a simple country girl who'd married the wrong guy when she was far too young to know what she was doing, become a widow soon after and finally met the love of her life. Her philosophy of toeing the line and listening to authority had always worked in her favor. But now another of her strongly held beliefs was causing her to throw all of that into question. An internal voice urging her to do the right thing.

Her father Buck talked often of sheeple and their tendency to exchange rights and freedoms for safety and security. The state of American society at present, like the air outside, had become toxic and dangerous. And everything in her being begged and pleaded with her to do whatever was necessary to keep from getting hurt. But she couldn't help wondering whether a life bought at such a high cost was one worth living.

Susan reached the bank of elevators, brought her trolley loaded with coolers to a stop and pressed the down arrow. As she waited, other scientists gathered beside her. Each of them had a name stitched onto their white lab coat and she stole quick glances, wondering whether any of them were Dennis Dresselhaus, the man Wendy had said would have answers to her questions.

She scanned the digital readout above the doors. Each of the elevators were on sublevel one, the same floor she and her trolley were headed to. Wendy had lent Susan her keycard so she could access the lower floors.

The crowd gathering around her began to grow, many tapping their feet and wondering out loud what was taking so long. Susan's pulse began to quicken. Maybe this wasn't such a good idea. Besides, who was this Dennis person she was searching for and how exactly did one begin that kind of conversation?

Hi, my name's Susan. Don't worry, Wendy already showed me the secret handshake. Do you have the microfilm? The mental image made her smile. She was being dramatic. Nothing foul was afoot in the Ark, apart from an overactive imagination.

At last, all three elevators arrived at once, and those assembled filed in. A single floor down, that was how far she was going and for some reason this high-tech box seemed to be taking forever. Suddenly that strange feeling of increased g-forces hit her as the elevator came to a stop. The doors opened and Susan got off, pushing her trolley, searching around like a kid on her first day of school.

She found herself in a brightly lit tunnel. Something about it reminded her of a spaceship, perhaps a corridor on the International Space Station. The analogy worked except for two noticeable differences. The first was the lack of zero gravity. The other was the metal grate flooring. The trolley rumbled over it as she went, making a racket.

Soon she came to an area divided by glass walls. Behind them, men and women wearing lab coats, blue gloves and small masks were hard at work.

This was biohazard level one, as Wendy had explained, the floor which housed the least lethal bacteria and viruses. If this was the kind of precautions they took here, she didn't want to know what things looked like three floors down.

Near the end of the hallway, a security guard approached her. She explained who she was and why she'd come. He told her he'd take the trolley and deliver it.

"I was told to speak with Dennis Dresselhaus."

The guard gave her a funny look. He was somewhere in his thirties, his face pockmarked, with a nose far too large for his face. "Who sent you?"

She hesitated, the blood draining from her face.

"I'm asking because Dr. Dresselhaus was just arrested."

Susan's heart nearly burst in her chest. "Arrested?"

"Yeah, the director's personal bodyguard came in and took him away."

Hand cupped over her mouth, Susan said: "I didn't even know he had a bodyguard."

"Secret Service men. But all this is above my pay grade."

"Was that why the elevators took so long?"

He nodded. "They had me shut down all of 'em till they'd carted him away."

"I can't believe it." Susan's mind was spinning in a million different directions. "Do you know why?"

115

"They only said they wanted to ask him a few questions. But I won't lie. Dr. Dresselhaus was about to pee his pants. A man who has nothing to hide shouldn't be that nervous."

"I guess not." Susan turned to leave.

"Hey, if he ever comes back I'll tell him you were looking for him. What's your name?"

Susan stopped, hesitating. "Don't worry about it. I'll come back another time."

She couldn't get back into the elevator and up to the main lobby quick enough. The whole time the hairs on the back of her neck were standing on end. Had her conversation with Wendy somehow been responsible? Or was this just some terrible coincidence?

The answer to her question arrived as she returned to the infirmary and saw the commotion. Autumn ran up to her, practically in tears. "The police just came and arrested one of the nurses," she stammered. And Susan didn't need to hear the woman's name to know who Autumn was talking about. Wendy had been right when she'd said the Ark was operating under its own set of rules.

Susan removed Wendy's keycard from around her neck and discreetly threw it into a trash bin. They were no longer in the America she knew. This was a new land, run by a man who called himself a director but was in truth something far worse.

Chapter 23

Paul returned to their apartment in Ark One, feeling like a man who'd just been soundly beaten by Bobby Fischer in a chess tournament. The similar look of defeat on Buck's face had stayed with him until the two had parted ways by the Park. It was clear the old guy needed some time. Paul supposed he was sitting on a bench somewhere, soaking in the artificial sunlight, wondering how Van Buren had known so much about them.

It was a good question and one Paul had asked himself more than once. More surprising was that the two of them hadn't been arrested. If there was such a thing as a guardian angel, then one was surely looking over their shoulder.

Paul closed the apartment door behind him and found Susan sitting at the table. The room was dark except for the warm glow from a hanging light above her. Judging by the pained expression on her face, she must have heard about their arrest.

She looked up, distant, making him suddenly wonder if he'd been wrong.

"I'm guessing you heard?" he probed.

Her sad eyes found him in the gloom. "Heard?"

"Our arrest. Buck punched a congressman's assistant. Got us both hauled up before Van Buren."

She shook her head. "Was he okay?"

"Who, Buck?"

"No, the assistant."

Paul grinned. "Hope not. Buck laid him out cold. Couldn't believe it."

She didn't seem all that interested.

"Hey, did you know your father was dishonorably discharged from the military?"

Almost in response, her fingers closed around a scrap of paper in her hand.

"What's that?" For the first time he noticed Susan was fighting back tears. "Has someone been hurt?" he asked, feeling panic grip him. "Where's Autumn?"

"Autumn's fine, Paul. But I think I may have put us in danger and I'm feeling sick to my stomach."

Paul came forward and curled an arm around her. "What happened?"

She told him about the vials, about her talk with Wendy and how the senior nurse and Dr. Dresselhaus had both been arrested.

"What for?"

"I don't know for sure, but it must have something to do with our conversation. There's nothing else it could be."

"But no one came after you."

Her head sank. "Not yet." Susan held out the crumpled scrap of paper.

Paul took it.

118

"When I came in I found this. Someone must have slipped it under the door."

Flattening the paper on the table, he scanned the handwritten note, pulse thumping in his neck.

"Your lives are in danger. DO AS YOU'RE TOLD!"

Those last words shouted off the page.

"Did you see anyone suspicious when you came home?" he asked, playing detective.

"No, everything was normal. A man passed me in the hallway, but he was a civilian. I've seen him here since day one and he barely looked in my direction."

"You never know who's capable of such a thing."

"Becoming paranoid isn't the solution," she answered, wiping her eyes. "I'm scared, Paul. I'm frightened and feeling terrible inside, like I did something wrong and now innocent people are going to pay the price."

"Honey, you didn't do anything wrong. You asked a question. Has that become a chargeable offense in the last week?"

She glanced up at him as if to say, *Maybe it has.*

"Well, that's not the kinda country I wanna live in and I can assure you it isn't the sort Buck wants either. The real question is, how did they know what Wendy told you?"

Susan shrugged her shoulders. "She seemed really scared when the subject came up. To the point where I closed the door so no one would overhear us. I can't imagine she would have gone and opened her mouth to the wrong person."

"You mentioned bugs the other day," he said thoughtfully. "Maybe you were right."

"Really?" She seemed to be having a hard time buying the idea. "It's just hardly a likely place to plant a listening device. Hardly anyone goes in there except to store vaccines."

119

A horrible thought bloomed in Paul's mind just then and the implications chilled his blood. He pointed an index finger to his ear and then to the ceiling.

She flinched.

Taking her by the arm, he ushered her out and into the hallway, leading her to a fire escape at the end of the corridor. Once in the stairwell, Paul felt like he could breathe again.

"Whoever wrote this note wants to keep us quiet," Paul said.

"Quiet? You know what I want? I wanna pack up and leave right away." Susan's eyes were searching around the concrete surroundings, checking to see if it was safe to talk.

"You know we can't do that."

"The radiation levels are down today. We might be able to make it." There was a note of desperation in her voice.

"Not low enough, we'd never make it, even wearing suits."

She cupped her head. "Then what other choice do we have but to do what the note says?"

He hated hearing her cave in to threats. Paul wasn't a scrapper. In many ways, getting along in peaceful coexistence was his goal in life. Battling the powers that be, that was Buck's game, and right now the old war bear was in the Park licking his wounds.

"I have this strange feeling someone is watching out for us," Paul told her. "We've run into more than enough trouble to get us kicked out of the Ark several times over and yet here we are."

"You're not talking about divine intervention."

He laughed. "No. I'm talking about a flesh-and-blood person. Someone who knows that what's going on in here is wrong."

"So what are you saying?"

"I'm saying we need to find them before things get out of hand."

Chapter 24

A short time later, Paul and Susan found Buck in the park, seated on a bench next to the pond. He was tossing pieces of bread to a paddling of ducks, looking like he didn't want to be bothered.

"You know they're genetically engineered to like humans," Paul offered as they drew near.

Buck glanced up and grunted. "Why else would they be spending time with a lout like me?"

"I've never known you to feel sorry for yourself, Dad," Susan said, startled.

He threw a handful in and the ducks scurried after it. "I'll bet there's a lot about me you don't know."

"We're here if you wanna talk about it," she offered, sitting next to him.

"Talking does nothing besides waste oxygen. 'Sides, the two of you look like you're up to something and I'm not sure I want any part of it."

Susan cleared her throat and couldn't get the words out before Paul jumped in.

"Something, uh, strange is going on in the bunker."

Buck let out an ironic burst of laughter. "You're only seeing that now? Heck, that ain't no newsflash."

Susan told him about the vials and how both medical personnel had been arrested.

"Any particular reason they're so keen to shoot salt water into people's bodies?" the old man asked.

"None that we've been able to figure out," Paul told him.

"I can't stand the idea of doctors coming at me with needles. And I like the idea of vaccinations even less."

Paul crossed his arms. "Yes, we know."

"Then you should know I'm done taking 'em." Buck turned to Susan. "And you can tell that handsome doctor of yours to his face."

Paul gave her a look.

"What?" she said, stepping back. "He's a good-looking man. I'm married, not dead."

Now it was his turn to wonder. "I fear the woman doth protest too much." His gaze returned to Buck. "As for announcing your decision to stop taking inoculations, I'm sure the powers that be are already aware of that."

Buck's forehead scrunched up. "How so?"

"We think there's a listening device in our room," Susan told him. "Maybe one in every room."

Her father shot a glance over his shoulder, scrutinizing a bush and a majestic oak behind them.

"Yes," Paul said, half joking. "The trees and shrubs may be wired as well."

"Don't doubt it. The more I hear the two of you talk, the more I'm convinced this place is being run by the Illuminati."

"Oh, no," Paul spat. "Not more conspiracy nonsense. Buck, this is serious."

"And so am I, Rock Star. Just think about who's in charge of this place. He ain't in the service. But he is part of what Eisenhower warned about—the military-industrial complex."

Paul's greatest concern bringing Buck into the fold was that the conversation would devolve into the stuff you found on bad websites. Crazy theories with nothing but scraps of misinformation to prop them up.

"I wasn't the one who thought of it first," Buck was saying. "Earl Mullins brought a few facts to my attention I hadn't even considered. Take, for example, the layout of this place."

Paul and Susan surveyed the Park, both looking confused.

"The Illuminati's main symbol is a pyramid with an all-seeing eye in the middle."

"Okay…" Paul said, dragging out the word, hoping Buck would get to the point.

"Just take a look at Arks One, Two and Three." He pulled out a hand-drawn map from his back pocket and spread it over his lap. "They're configured in the shape of a pyramid with the Park smack dab in the middle representing the eye."

Susan was nodding.

"Oh, come on," Paul said. "That isn't proof of anything, Buck, apart from an architectural coincidence."

"Call it a coincidence if you want, but I've been feeling like this place wasn't right from the start. They tell us we're free to go, but walking out into certain death ain't really freedom."

Paul didn't think this conversation was heading in the right direction. "Listen, I believe that someone on the inside may be looking out for us," he said, trying to change the subject. "They may be keeping us from being kicked out."

124

"Well, quite frankly, I wish they'd stop," Buck said. "I'm starting to think maybe we should leave and take our chances out there."

"You may be willing to throw your own life away," Paul replied. "But what about Autumn? Is her future that disposable?" His voice was starting to rise and Susan placed a gentle hand on his back.

Buck seemed to be pondering Paul's last words. "I got no beef finding the person on the inside. Maybe they can help fill in a few blanks and help us figure out what's going on in here. But no matter how we go about it, that corporate stooge Van Buren and his personal assistant, Ava Monroe, can't find out what we're up to."

The faint sound of a commotion echoed from the far end of the park. It was coming from the airlock near Ark Three, the administrative and governmental wing. They rose quickly and headed in that direction. If there was some kind of emergency, they didn't want to be the last ones to find out about it. As they drew closer, a few dozen people were pushing to get into the airlock.

"What's going on?" Buck demanded.

A young girl with pigtails spun around, her face filled with amazement.

"The president's arrived."

Chapter 25

The three struggled into the airlock, Paul moving slowly as he excused himself, Buck ahead of him using elbows and his weight to plow his way through. The lights went from red to green and the hatch at the other end opened up and suddenly they were fighting the crowd all over again. It wasn't even clear why everyone was in such a hurry. Did they really believe a savior had arrived to make their lives better?

At last, they made it into the atrium of Ark Three in time to see the president arrive, surrounded by a veritable army of Secret Service agents and what were likely White House personnel. Paul was struck immediately by the new president's height. He couldn't have been more than five foot two with a full head of silver hair trimmed into a businessman's cut, short on the sides, the top just long enough to part. He smiled and waved and the civilians dressed in their earth-toned tunics shouted and cheered. For a brief moment the country wasn't falling to pieces, nuclear devices hadn't vaporized hundreds of thousands of citizens and deadly radiation wasn't poisoning all it came in contact with. The saviour had arrived and by his very presence he would set everything right again. Even Paul found himself clapping and whistling. Only Buck was booing and hissing, a response that even the president's Secret Service agents seemed to notice, some of them pointing in their direction.

"What are you, dumb?" Paul shouted over the jubilation.

"He's a usurper," Buck yelled back.

"Maybe, but now's not the time to draw attention."

Van Buren and Ava were there to greet him. It was as though Air Force One had just touched down and the dignitaries were there to say hello. Without a doubt, the new president's entrance had been choreographed, the way every little bit of politics was nowadays. *This is your new leader,* was the message, and a man like Van Buren was surely eager to get the point across.

Buck's fists were still clenched as President Perkins passed, shaking hands as he did so. Buck's elbowing technique had gotten them right to the front of the crowd and now here they were in a kind of presidential receiving line. Shadowed by his agents, Perkins moved along shaking hand after hand, even offering the occasional fist bump so the kids knew he was a cool customer and not some crusty old guy.

Perkins arrived before Paul, who held out his hand. The president took it with his left and pumped it twice, reaching past him with his right to a woman standing behind them.

"I love you!" she shouted, leaving Paul to wonder if he was in some kind of bizarro world.

Buck was next and he stood there, arms at his sides, hands curled into fists. The president reached out, his hand seeming to hang in the air for an eternity. Time slowed as the Secret Service agents zoomed in to what was happening, or rather what wasn't happening.

Don't be an idiot, Buck, Paul kept thinking over and over, hoping his thoughts might somehow penetrate the old man's impossibly thick skull. This wasn't the time to make a stand and draw the wrath of the powers that be.

Paul's heart was pounding against his ribcage as the president's expression changed. His agents stepped forward, and that was when Buck at last took his hand and shook it.

"Glad you arrived safely," Buck said, his voice low and raspy.

President Perkins smiled, not entirely sure what had just happened. "Trust me, you don't want to go outside. The weather's a real killer."

He moved on after that, pushing down the line until he cut back and went to Van Buren, who'd stood there waiting patiently. They exchanged pleasantries. Some members of the president's entourage were taking pictures. Shots which would surely grace an exhibit in a museum decades from now.

Then the presidential mob moved away, disappearing into the bowels of Ark Three, leaving Paul to wonder what these men would talk about next, when the cameras and the average citizens weren't there to hear them.

Over in the mess hall of Ark One, Autumn and Brett were locked in a passionate embrace. She pulled away, unable to wipe the smile off her face.

"You know if my grandfather caught us, he'd kill you."

Brett looked visibly concerned. "He's a scary man."

"Sort of. But deep down he's really a big ol' teddy bear."

"The bear part I believe, I'm not so sure about the teddy part though."

They laughed and he went to kiss her again before stopping short. A smattering of civilians were nearby, seated at tables and chatting. Dinner wasn't for another hour and many of them had probably recently finished a shift in whatever line of work they'd been conscripted to perform.

"What's wrong?" Autumn asked.

"I was wondering why you mentioned your grandfather being upset. Most girls warn you about their dads."

Her chin dropped. "Most girls?"

Brett blushed and tried to backtrack. "You know what I mean."

"I don't know. I guess my dad's kinda laid-back. Sometimes I wish he'd been a little stricter. Sounds weird to say it, but I do."

"Not weird at all," Brett told her. An eyelash was on her cheek and he blew it away. "It woulda made you feel more protected."

"Who wouldn't want the freedom to do whatever they wanted? But there's something about boundaries that help. Sorta like the Ark."

That got his attention. He was still wearing his fatigues and she straightened his collar as he asked her to explain what she meant.

"Well, there are clearly rules in here people must follow, but if they don't, not much happens."

"Really?"

"A friend of my grandfather's named Earl or something didn't think he or his family ought to work and left in the middle of the night."

Brett's eyes dropped.

"Trust me," she assured him. "That's the last thing I'd want to happen. In fact, the very idea terrifies me."

"If they wanted to go, would you follow them?" he asked her.

She hesitated and then took his hand. "I really like it here."

"Me too." He swallowed. "But there's something I have to tell you."

"It's not something bad, I hope."

"Your dad and Grampa Buck have been stirring up a lot of trouble lately."

"Why doesn't that surprise me?" she said, trying to laugh it off.

"I'm serious. I've had to vouch for them on a couple of different occasions, but I'm worried I don't have any more get-out-of-jail-free cards. You need to talk to them. Explain how important it is that they fall in line. If I was a higher rank, my word might have more weight, but as it is…" His voice fell off. "I'm worried something terrible might happen and all of you will be punished."

"I won't leave, Brett. I know I wasn't clear when you asked me the first time, but I want to stay here, at least until things get better out there. Then we can decide what's best."

"No, I don't think you understand." He was emphatic and the tone of his voice was making her nervous. "This isn't about packing your things and going away. If there's one thing about the Ark you need to understand, it's that no matter what they tell you, no one leaves here alive."

Chapter 26

The following morning, Paul and Buck headed off to work, a cloud still hanging over them. A digital readout on the wall by the elevator told them the air outside continued to be deadly, leaving both men to wonder if this had become the new normal. The mood the evening before had been quiet and subdued. Even Autumn, who was normally full of energy and eager to discuss anything and everything Brett-related, had little to say.

Donning their now dirty yellow coveralls, the two men assembled for the assignment of daily responsibilities. Today was their turn to push the giant collector bins around, gathering trash from the other maintenance workers and bringing it to the incinerator on sublevel one of Ark Two. That meant they would spend the day stinking of garbage since they would need to dump the trash into sorting piles before being burned. Nothing that could be reused would go to waste. Before someone threw out a tube of toothpaste, it had to be squeezed dry. A comb missing a few bristles could still be used. It was nasty work for sure, but Paul saw a certain amount of logic in it.

Paul and Buck signed out their collector bins and set to work in the atrium, following maintenance workers ready to offload what they'd already gathered.

But their silence had a more practical reason: the possible presence of listening devices in their room. Generally speaking, the mood among the civilians inside the Ark was at an all-time high and Paul expected much of that had to do with the arrival of the president. The unspoken expectation was that his arrival might signal a shift in the growing inequalities.

A short loud-mouthed Italian worker named Gabby stopped to offload his container into Paul's bin.

"I don't know," Gabby said, with the slightest hint of a New Jersey accent. "I kinda expected him to be taller." That last word he pronounced 'tallah'.

Buck glanced over and kept on going, not wanting to waste another second talking about a leader he considered illegitimate.

"I see what you mean," Paul replied. "Now we gotta wait and see how he shakes things up around here."

Gabby's face lit up. "First things first, he better end these work details. I mean, what are we, a buncha slaves?"

"Not us," Paul said, not believing a word of it.

A final bag of trash flung into the bin and Gabby was off, leaving Paul to wonder if anyone here had any idea what was really going on. There wouldn't be any changes, at least none in the direction they were hoping for.

He crossed the atrium and caught up with Buck.

"How's your load?"

Buck smacked the side of his bin, listening for the echo. "Sounds like she's about half full."

Almost on cue, a maintenance worker appeared and offloaded another bag.

"Make that three-quarters," Buck amended.

"Listen, I've been meaning to ask you about something."

Buck suddenly looked unsure.

"Your dishonorable discharge."

Groaning, Buck kept pushing his bin.

"Listen, I get you don't wanna talk about it, but you know there's a lot about each other we don't know."

"And I'd like to keep it that way," Buck snapped.

Paul smiled and tried to keep up. The bin was getting harder to push. "I've got something I want to confess," he told his father-in-law.

"If it's got anything to do with dressing in women's clothes, I don't wanna hear it."

"What? Of course not. Buck, I don't even know where you get these ideas." Paul collected himself. "In the 2000 presidential election, I voted for George W Bush."

Buck stopped cold.

"I know, it's hard to believe, but I did."

"A dyed-in-the-wool liberal from the far left like yourself?" Buck said in shock. "I'm speechless."

"Fifth-generation liberal, I might add, although I wouldn't say I'm far left."

"I know about your past. You're far left."

The two men continued through the atrium. "When I was younger, that might have been true. But this is my point, Buck. As a man gets older, he tends to see the world in a different light."

"That so? What about 2004?" Buck asked.

Paul grinned. "Same. Listen, when I saw George W, able to cast doubt on John Kerry's bravery, a decorated war hero, and Kerry didn't fight back, well, I realized right then this wasn't the kind of guy I wanted at the helm."

The subject of war heroes wiped the grin off Buck's lips. He grew quiet for a moment. Two more workers dumped their trash and now both bins were full. They turned and headed for the lift and sublevel one where they would sort and burn what they'd collected.

"That discharge wasn't what it looks like," Buck said. "A quaint little village in the Iron Triangle called Ben Suc. I was with the 1st Infantry. About thirty thousand American forces in all. 173rd Airborne Brigade, 11th Armored Cav among others. We were out on an operation codenamed Cedar Falls. The objective was to encircle and destroy the Viet Cong and North Vietnamese regulars in the area. Deny them bases from which to launch attacks. Safe havens, we call 'em now. Major-General William DePuy was our commander. Short man with a slight build, normally the kinda person I don't have much use for, but this guy had cojones the size of cantaloupes. A real scrapper. See, I thought we were going in to kick some Commie butt. That's what I'd signed on for. Turns out we hardly found any butts worth kicking. Most musta heard the attack was coming and fled the area. And that's when things started turning ugly. A major phase of the operation involved taking locals into custody for resettlement and burning their villages to the ground. Stories started circling around about atrocities, soldiers taking out their frustrations on innocent civilians. My platoon had already reduced two villages to ash when we were ordered to hit a third and that was when something inside me just snapped."

Both men were standing by the elevators, Paul hanging on his every word.

"Went up to DePuy myself and told him I wasn't gonna do it. That it was wrong. These people were innocent and we were only making ourselves look worse than the Viet Cong we'd sworn to destroy. Even with a French name like DePuy, our commander wasn't a hothead. He made it real clear. Get back in there and destroy those villages and put the inhabitants into camps or face a court martial."

"So what'd you do?"

"I went to jail, Paul. That is until a media firestorm blew up bigger than an atom bomb over the whole campaign. They knew a court martial would only draw more negative attention and turn me into a martyr, so they set me free. The next day I was given a dishonorable discharge."

The elevator doors opened and with some difficulty, both men squeezed their bins inside.

"But how could you be ashamed? You did the right thing."

Buck scoffed as he tapped sublevel one with the side of his fist. "I suppose it depends which end of the barrel you were looking down. The left-wing hippies approved, but the truth was I disobeyed orders."

Shaking his head, Paul said: "You never could take being told what to do. You stood up for what you believed in." He paused. "If you could go back, what would you have done differently?"

Buck regarded him thoughtfully. "I called foul after our platoon had already torched two villages. As far as I'm concerned, that was two too many."

Chapter 27

The elevator doors opened onto a corridor. Arrows on the wall before them pointed in both directions. To the left was Waste Management and beneath that words in bold red lettering: Restricted Access. To the right was Trash Incineration. Two men in purple coveralls, white keycards clipped to their breast pockets, were waiting to head back up. Their purple outfits along with their access to restricted areas signaled that they had seniority and high-level clearance.

Grunting from the strain of pushing the heavy bins, Paul and Buck exited, heading to the right.

"What do you think they were doing?" he asked Buck after the men in purple disappeared into the elevator.

"How should I know?"

"I just don't see why the Waste Management area would be restricted."

"That's simple," Buck said, coming to a pair of swing doors and pushing them open with the front of his bin. "They don't want anyone messing with the pipes. You know, backing up toilets. Besides, what's one more secret area in a place like this?"

Upon entering, they came to an open pit where the trash was emptied and sorted with the help of other workers in yellow coveralls. From there it was placed on conveyer belts which fed it into one of three furnaces. Part of the heat generated was apparently fed back into the system. It was designed to maximize efficiency, but it didn't do much to keep the place from smelling awful. After an hour of this, Paul and Buck headed back toward the elevator.

As they waited, Paul stood staring down the corridor, willing the Waste Management doors to swing open so he could get a glimpse of what was going on in there.

When the elevator arrived this time, two different workers in purple appeared, each behind a smaller, open-topped bin. Inside were what looked like old towels and scraps of torn beige cloth. One of the men swore as the wheel of his container got jammed in the gap between the lift and the floor. He yanked it back and tried again, a thick vein in his forehead protruding. Buck stepped in to help him. The trick was to pull the bins out rather than push them from behind. Buck grabbed hold of the sides and pulled. With a jerk, the bin shot forward and over the elevator lip.

A human hand rose up from beneath the pile of shredded cloth and hung in the air for a moment— discolored fingers curled into a claw—before settling back out of view.

The whole thing hadn't lasted more than a split second, short enough that neither of the men in purple had noticed a thing. But Buck had and so too had Paul.

The workers in purple nodded in thanks and went off down the narrow corridor, the wheels of their plastic bins echoing as they faded in the distance.

"I know I ain't going crazy," Buck said, slowly.

"If that was an illusion then we're both going nuts."

Buck's hand hovered over the button to recall the elevator. "People die," he said.

"Every day," Paul added.

"That's right, every day, and when they do their bodies need to be disposed of."

"Uh-huh. Can't be buried. Not here."

"Burned. That's what I was thinking too." His finger inched closer to calling the elevator. Buck's finger did a little dance before he pulled it away. "Can't shake the feeling that was something neither of us were meant to see. People who die aren't carted away under a heap of old rags."

"Your logic is sound," Paul said. "Shall we?" he asked, aiming a finger down the corridor at the restricted area labelled Waste Management.

"We shall," Buck said, squaring his shoulders and leading the way.

And as they set out, Paul couldn't help remembering those villages in Vietnam Buck had told him about. How so many had simply done what they were told to do. Had he been present, Paul might have done the same. Followed orders and destroyed the lives of innocent people. But that was before he'd known Buck. Before he'd seen there was another way.

Chapter 28

A small janitor's closet at the end of the hall stood less than ten feet from the double doors securing the Waste Management area.

Paul stopped and tried the door handle. It was open and he let himself inside.

"What're you doing in there?" Buck barked. The old man was standing by the double doors, examining the keypad.

"Unless you know the code to get in," Paul replied, "I suggest we hide in here until those two come out. We might be able to catch the door before it shuts."

Buck gave one last look at the keypad and grunted. With obvious reluctance, he followed Paul's advice and both men squeezed into the small closet. Inside was a mop bucket, a hose jutting out from the wall and shelves filled with cleaning products.

Buck's large girth meant there was even less room. The stale air reeked of bleach and Pine-Sol.

"I think the military owes you an apology," Paul said, trying to break the uneasy silence.

"They don't owe me a darn thing."

"Well, that's not fair. You stood up for what was right."

Buck chuckled. "No one ever said life was fair."

A sound from outside. The clanging of doors swinging open. Buck opened the door less than an inch and peered out. The two men in purple were pushing their now empty containers through the doorway. When they moved out of sight, he moved fast but silently and caught one of the double doors before it closed, waving at Paul to follow.

A moment later they were inside, both of them not entirely sure what they were about to see. They soon found themselves moving down a long tunnel, thick steel pipes overhead, heat hitting them in waves. Another group of men in purple coveralls might appear behind them at any moment. If there was anything to see here, they'd have to find it fast.

Heart racing, Paul took the lead. Soon, they reached a set of swivel doors, each centered with a small porthole. They peered through and what they saw made the breath catch in their throats. A dozen men in purple sorting through mountains of personal possessions, tossing items left and right into smaller piles. Watches, pants, t-shirts, pots and pans, paintings, silverware. The list went on and on. It didn't take long for Paul to realize what he was seeing. These objects had once belonged to the civilians living in the Ark. These were the things they'd been forbidden from bringing inside. Now they were being inventoried like war booty.

He and Buck exchanged a look. Further down they saw more swing doors and headed in that direction.

There, the sight was even more disturbing. In the corner of another sorting room was a wheelchair that Paul recognized. It had belonged to the woman he'd seen in the park. She'd been exempted from work duties and he hadn't seen her or her husband after that. At the time, Paul hadn't thought much of it. The truth was he'd had his own troubles to worry about, but now the thought of what had become of them made him sick.

On a table nearby, other disturbing items were stacked. Mounds of false teeth, leg braces and then a prosthetic arm he'd seen before.

He pointed, his finger shaking. "Didn't that belong to Earl Mullins' son?"

Then further along, barely out of sight, they saw a row of furnaces where men in purple were stuffing bodies inside.

They'd been told those unable to work would get a pass, that Earl and his family had been allowed to leave, but now it was clear all that had been a lie.

The only anyone ever left the Ark was through the chimney.

Chapter 29

President Perkins found Victor Van Buren's office warm and inviting, a stark contrast to the man himself. The overall impression was that the room had been carved from a block of stained mahogany. Behind the eighteenth-century Chippendale desk were bookshelves which reached fifteen feet to the ceiling. A single ladder sat on a brass track that ran the length of the room.

Van Buren reclined in the tufted brown leather chair, framed by a print of Van Gogh's famous painting Irises.

"Drink?" Van Buren asked, following Perkins' gaze.

The president shook his head.

"You're wondering about the painting," Van Buren said, rising from his seat. It was a flower bed of irises. A single white flower stood out among a sea of violets. He grinned. "You're far too polite to ask if it's an original."

Perkins laughed and shifted in his chair.

"I bought it from the Getty six months ago. A priceless work of art. I paid an arm and a leg for it, you know."

"I'm sure you did."

"Were you aware that Van Gogh painted it in an asylum the year before his death?"

"No, I wasn't."

"Not many are." Van Buren ran his fingers over the canvas. "Each of the flowers is unique. Van Gogh studied every contour and shape to capture a variety of curved silhouettes. The overflowing borders are influenced by Japanese woodblock prints."

"It's beautiful."

"One of his best," Van Buren said as he opened his desk drawer, removed a box cutter and swung it, slashing the painting.

Perkins stood, alarmed. "What are you doing?"

Van Buren brought the blade down again, cutting so deep he scored a chunk out of the wall behind it. After a few more frenzied moments he stopped, his white hair out of place. With the palm of his hand, he fixed his coif and sat down and replaced the box cutter.

Perkins was standing now, eyes wide and fearful. "Why did you do that? You said yourself it was priceless."

"It was, Edmund," Van Buren assured him. "One of a kind and I did it to make a point."

"I don't understand."

"That if need be, I'm perfectly at ease destroying something beautiful. Especially when something better is set to take its place."

Van Buren was referring to the country. But did he need to nearly give Perkins a heart attack to make that point? And hadn't he proven himself in this regard already? They were here after all, which meant the plan had worked, the cost in human lives be damned.

That last word was one Perkins had thought of often these days. They would be damned for what they'd done.

"Those congressmen and senators shuffling about on the floors beneath us don't know you've enacted Executive Directive 51, do they?" Van Buren asked, dusting flecks of paint off his shoulders.

"Not yet, but they will soon. That's what took me so long to get here. Tying up loose ends."

ED51, signed into law in 2007 by Bush, essentially bestowed full executive powers on the president in the event of a catastrophic event. The aim was to facilitate the continuity of government, but in effect it facilitated the creation of a dictatorship. All they needed was a catastrophe.

"Why am I getting the overwhelming feeling you're having second thoughts?" Van Buren opened his desk drawer, removed a silver coin and began deftly flipping it over his knuckles. Another one of his magic tricks.

Perkins' eyes fell to the floor. "How can anyone ever be prepared for something like this? So many people have died."

"And so will many more. Eventually, we'll all be dead, Edmund. Is that what's got you scared, death?"

"Of course not."

"You knew what you were getting involved in."

"I know…"

Van Buren set the coin down and steepled his fingers. "Have I ever told you about Jocelyn?"

Perkins glanced up. "I don't think you have."

"She was my only daughter," Van Buren said. "A lovely girl. Smart as a fox with a head for business. She was twenty when we discovered she had a rare, incurable blood disorder. Like all parents, my first response was shock, then disbelief. But unlike most parents I had billions at my disposal and I threw the weight of my considerable fortune into finding a cure. Donations to research and pleas to politicians came to nothing as I watched my daughter wither away. It was about that time that the anger began to settle in. How was it, with all my resources, that I couldn't save my daughter's life? I was at a biomedical conference in Switzerland when I heard the news about Jocelyn's passing."

Perkins exhaled loudly. "Oh, no."

"I'd been so focused on finding a cure, I hadn't even been by her side during those final days and hours."

"You never gave up."

"That's right, but one good thing did come of my trip. A great thing in fact. I met a gentleman at the conference in Zurich named Samuel Rutledge."

"The oil tycoon?"

"That's the one," Van Buren said. "But I was less interested in what he had to say about the future of arctic drilling than I was in the ring on his finger. I saw it when we shook hands. A simple band with a triangle centered with an eye. He said it had something to do with the Bilderberg Group, but wouldn't say more. A secret society of wealthy businessmen, that was all I knew.

"Over the succeeding months, I peppered him with a barrage of letters and phone calls until he finally relented. I suppose in my grief, I needed something new to channel my energies into. Then one night I received a phone call from a man I'd never spoken to before. He gave me an address in New York City and told me to be there at eight sharp the following evening. He then proceeded to give me a list of instructions. Things I wasn't supposed to do between now and then. I couldn't eat or drink any alcohol and, most importantly, I had to come alone. The following day, I took a private jet to JFK and did as the man instructed. To say I wasn't nervous would have been a lie, but I saw no reason not to trust Samuel Rutledge.

"I didn't know it then, but I was being brought to an initiation ceremony. What I witnessed that night was strange and frightening and I was strictly forbidden from discussing it with anyone. Suffice it to say, I was inducted into a brotherhood whose power and influence were far greater than I could ever have imagined. I'd only wished I'd discovered them sooner. Maybe then my Jocelyn could have lived." His glassy eyes met Perkins'. "That was twenty years ago and over that time, I've worked my way up within the organization to become its leader. Which was why I reached out to you when you were nothing but an outmatched wannabe congressman."

"You helped to get me elected," Perkins said. "I owe you for that, I know."

"This isn't about owing," Van Buren said. "This is about scooping the country up off its feet and making it great again. Don't you want to make it great?"

"I do," Perkins said and he meant it.

Van Buren's silver coin was out again, jumping from one finger to the next. "Then never forget. From chaos comes order, a new world order."

Perkins nodded.

"Do you like parties?" Van Buren asked.

The director never called him Mr. President. Even after Perkins had attained that lofty position, there was still a power differential between the two men.

"Who doesn't?"

"The morale in the Ark's been rather low lately. With the second phase of Project Genesis officially underway, I think it's only fitting that we organize a celebration."

Chapter 30

Working her way through the airlock and into the Park, Susan didn't waste any time looking for Buck. He'd left her a note in the room, telling her to meet him here. She could only guess her father was with Paul since the two men had been nearly inseparable these last few days.

The Park was busy, making Susan's task all the more difficult. Couples in beige civilian tunics strolled hand in hand next to families sitting down for a picnic beneath a row of evergreens. Not far away, a child squealed with joy as he played with a Pitbull genetically modified to never bite him. It was a strange world they were living in, but more amazing was how easily the folks here had adapted to it. That was one of the greatest strengths of our species, she thought philosophically, and also one of our greatest weaknesses. We often adapted to incremental changes, even when they laid the groundwork for our demise.

After a few more minutes of searching, Susan finally spotted Buck, standing next to a large boulder with two men. As she approached, she realized that neither of them was Paul.

"There you are," Buck said with his usual lack of patience. He looked sweaty and anxious. "You know Jeb and Allan."

"Of course. We thought you'd left."

Jeb flashed a gap-toothed grin. "We made the mistake of lettin' them know we used to be mechanics."

"They've had us down in the depths of Ark Two working on the backup diesel generators," Allan continued. He still had a smear of grease across his forehead to prove it. "Buck says he had something important to tell us, but wanted to wait till you was here."

"What about Paul?"

"He ran off to fetch Autumn," Buck said, shaking his head. "He's been gone a while now. Giving that guy a job to do is like playing the lotto. You hope it's gonna happen, but you're always ready for a disappointment."

"Be nice, Buck."

"Ain't no time to be nice." The old man looked around again. "Paul can fill Autumn in on his own. I'm just gonna lay it out."

Buck spent the next few minutes describing in detail what they had seen in the Waste Management area. The sorting rooms, the bodies being fed into furnaces and the murder of innocent people.

"Earl and his whole family," Jeb exclaimed, touching his forehead with fingers swollen from age and years of manual labor.

Susan felt the Park and the people in it begin to spin. She shot out a hand, gripping Buck's thick shoulder. He caught her before she could fall.

"I don't wanna believe it," she said, her breathing still shallow.

"Neither do I," Buck said. "But everything I told you is the truth. They're killing people who can't work, people who cause problems, and it probably won't be long before they start adding to that list."

"We need to get outta here as soon as possible," Susan told them, a thought that was clearly on everyone's mind.

"That's the problem," Buck replied with disgust. "This place is locked down tighter than Fort Knox. Ain't no way they're gonna open those giant steel doors just 'cause we ask politely. When I thought that Earl and his family had been allowed to leave it gave me a touch of hope. An ace up my sleeve. And I figured we could always follow suit and do the same if push came to shove, radiation or no radiation." He turned to the two men. "But neither of you two can breathe a word of this either. Don't mention it in your rooms either 'cause they're bugged."

"What the heck kinda place is this?"

"It's an evil place," Susan told them. "Masquerading as the Garden of Eden." Then something hit her. "What about the others?"

"Which others?" Buck replied.

Susan waved her hands around to the dozens of civilians enjoying the Park and the manmade sunlight overhead.

"You're starting to sound like that bleeding-heart husband of yours."

"Dad, leaving them here to be killed is just as bad as killing them ourselves."

She could see the battle going on behind Buck's eyes. His intense need for self-preservation was in a cage match against the empathy he tried so hard to deny.

"You're asking me to risk my family to save a bunch of people I barely know?"

Jeb and Allan were watching the back-and-forth like a tennis match.

"How can we plan an escape and leave everyone else behind? Could you really live with yourself knowing they may all be killed?"

Buck swore. "Why do you always need to complicate things with morality?"

The old man and Susan were still having it out when Paul showed up.

"About time," Buck snapped. "You stop for a snow cone?"

"I was looking for Autumn when something strange happened," Paul told them.

Susan grabbed his arm. "Right now we don't need any more strange, Paul."

"Two Secret Service agents found me in the mess hall during my search and told me the president wanted to have a word."

"Have a word?" Buck said in disbelief. "Are the two of you pals or something?"

"I didn't think so. But they brought me into this tiny room, looked almost like an interrogation booth, and I was sure this was it. They knew Buck and I had seen something we shouldn't and he was going to have me choose from a list of horrible options."

"So what'd they say?" Susan demanded.

"The president said he'd been a big fan of The Wanderers."

Buck threw his hands into the air. "Oh, no."

"Said he was sad we'd broken up all those years back. Asked me for an autograph and then said he was putting together a little celebration and wanted me to be the headline act."

"Did you agree?" Susan asked.

"I didn't have a choice. I tried to tell him I was rusty and didn't remember the lyrics anymore, but he insisted. Wouldn't take no for an answer."

"You've got to be kidding me," Buck shouted. He wasn't just mad, he was seething. "Don't you see what you've done?"

"How was this my fault?"

"All that fancy-schmancy music stuff, I knew it'd come back to bite us in the big one. A tiny dollop of anonymity was the only thing we had going for us. Now that you're the president's new best friend, we won't be able to fart without him smelling it."

Paul swallowed hard. "There's more."

Buck froze, fighting back the eruption bubbling beneath the surface.

"After I agreed and they let me out, I found Autumn. I told her we were leaving the bunker as soon as possible, that it wasn't safe here, and she lost it. Said we were being unfair, that things were great here."

"You didn't tell her what we saw?" Buck said, throwing his arms up.

"How could I? We were in the atrium of Ark Three, dozens of government stiffs walking by. What was I supposed to say? 'Hey, honey, we need to motor it 'cause these maniacs are killing people?' I don't think that woulda gone over very well."

"So what'd she do?" Susan asked.

Paul sighed. "She ran off and I couldn't catch her. Right now she could be anywhere."

"Not anywhere," Susan said. "I know Autumn. She went to Brett."

Now Buck's rage was complete. "That's what you get with liberal parenting. Kids who think they know best." He ran his fingers down the front of his face. "I can't believe this is happening."

Paul spoke up. "How we raise our daughter is our business, Buck, not yours."

Jeb and Allan looked on, entranced, their jaws dropped.

"Sure it is. All I'm saying is when you let your kids run wild, don't be surprised if they wander off and get themselves into trouble."

"I bear a lot of the responsibility," Susan said. "Paul tried to discourage her relationship with Brett and I told him it was fine. I thought she needed a little distraction given the situation."

The features of Buck's face settled. "Listen, right now we need to figure out where to go from here."

The others were in the process of agreeing when a nurse showed up, startling them.

"Sorry to interrupt," she said, looking at Susan. "But you're needed in the infirmary."

"Do you know what for?" Susan asked, trying to mask her unease.

"We're rolling out a new inoculation and we need everyone on deck to help prepare."

"When will it be administered?" Paul asked.

"Tomorrow morning," she said. "After the celebration."

As the nurse walked away, the five stood staring at one another.

"This might not be such a bad thing," Buck suggested.

"Really?" Paul replied. "I thought you of all people hated getting inoculations."

"Oh, I do, but if they need Susan, that means they'll also need Autumn." He turned to Susan. "When she shows up, tread carefully. This may be our only shot at convincing her to come with us when we break outta here."

152

Chapter 31

Paul and Buck made it back to their room in Ark One in record time. The chances that Autumn would be here were slim, but they needed to check nevertheless. As Paul pushed the door open and stepped inside, something on the floor went skittering under one of the bunk beds.

"What was that?" he asked, flicking on the light.

"Huh?" Buck asked, heading straight for the bathroom to see if Autumn was there. The entire apartment—if you could call it that—was three to four hundred square feet tops. If Paul's daughter had been here, they would have known the minute they walked in.

Paul went to the bunk bed and dropped to the floor. Not to look for Autumn, but for whatever he'd kicked when they walked in.

And it didn't take long for him to find it. Reaching into a patch of shadow, he emerged with a USB drive.

"This yours?" he asked, holding it up to Buck.

The old man glanced over and shook his head. "Why would I have one of those?" He was running his fingers along the wall, tapping every so often.

"What on earth are you doing?" Paul asked.

"Searching for little critters," he replied and winked.

Paul's face fell in confusion.

"You know…" And Buck pointed at his left ear. He was referring to the bug they suspected was in here somewhere.

"Do you even know what you're doing?"

"Of course I do. You just think of a way to…" Buck made a walking motion with his index and middle finger, a sign for 'help us escape'.

Paul hoped he found that bug soon, 'cause talking like this was starting to feel silly. He headed to the computer and inserted the USB. No sooner had he done so than a series of letters began scrolling across the screen.

"Uh, Buck. I think the listening device is in the light switch."

"Don't be an idiot, Paul. No one puts a bug in a light…" Buck turned around and saw the same letters dancing across the computer's digital display.

Step One: Remove the bug from the light switch by the main entrance.

The two men looked at one another.

"Well, I'll be," Buck said, moving to the switch. "Hey, pass me a screwdriver or something."

Paul laughed. "Sorry, I don't have my toolbelt on me. You're gonna need to use your fingernail."

"I was worried you were gonna say that." Buck slid his thumbnail into the groove on the screw head, his face twisting in pain as he began rotating his wrist.

"There you go," Paul encouraged him. "You're getting it."

"Keep quiet or you're gonna get it. This hurts like hell."

Several agonizing rotations and a bloody thumbnail later, Buck was done. He removed the faceplate and plucked out a circular device attached to a tiny circuit board. He squeezed the bug between his fingers, crushing it, then turned to Paul. "Now what?"

Not sure, Paul hit the enter key. The screen changed once again, this time displaying the external drive along with a series of folders.

Paul read each folder name loud. "'Sugarloaf Mountain,' 'Bilderberg,' '9/11,' 'MKUltra,' 'Project Genesis.'"

"What the heck is all this?" Buck asked, wiping his bloody thumbnail with a piece of toilet paper.

"I'm not sure," Paul replied, feeling suddenly very nervous. "But whoever gave it to us knew exactly where the listening device was located."

"Click on '9/11,'" Buck said, as he came in for a closer look.

Inside the file were a number of emails from Van Buren to various men they'd never heard of. In one of the subject lines were the words: 'Lessons from the 9/11 test run.'

"We already anticipated the impact the attacks would have on the fabric of society," Van Buren wrote. "What we underestimated was how quickly the country would come together and recover from the trauma. One encouraging sign was the passage of the Patriot Act, which helped to prove how easily a nation could be controlled and manipulated into adopting totalitarian rule."

Other documents showed how the plan had been laid out months in advance.

"The trick," one of the reports sent to Van Buren wrote, "will be to make the hijackers believe they aren't being aided and abided by the Western interests."

"What is all this?" Paul wondered.

"It's a blueprint," Buck shot back without a moment's hesitation.

As they continued reading, a number of disturbing facts became increasingly clear. The Bilderberg Group and others like it were simply underlings in a shadow organization which went back hundreds of years. Over the centuries they'd been known by many names, but none had ever captured the totality of the secret cabal that controlled them. Victor Van Buren wasn't only a rich industrialist. He was the figurehead for this group, a group without name and without parallel, a group behind countless overthrown governments, bloody wars, assassinations and even 9/11. But it was the next few items on their resume that really left Paul and Buck speechless. The Spanish Flu of 1918, Ebola, SARS, H1N1 had all been engineered by these people. But the purpose wasn't to cause death and disorder. The purpose was to prune the population and to invoke fear and thereby to control.

"Do you think these guys had anything to do with the terrorist attacks that landed us here?" Paul asked, already worried about the answer.

"Haven't I been telling you that all along?" Buck shot back.

"Not really. You said this place was run by the Illuminati."

"Exactly."

"But this says those guys are only footmen in a larger shadow organization."

"Now you're mincing words." Buck looked past him at the screen. "Get out of there and click on 'Project Genesis.'"

No sooner had Paul done so than someone pounded on the door. The two men exchanged a frightened glance.

"Autumn?" Paul asked, in a squeaky voice.

"It's Ark security," a man barked from the other side. "Open up before we kick the door down."

Chapter 32

Over at the infirmary, Susan was returning with a trolley stacked with blue coolers, each displaying a sticker which read 'handle with care'. Stored inside was the vaccine they would be giving people tomorrow morning.

Down on biohazard level one, the lack of frantic activity had surprised her. Presumably this was where the vaccine was manufactured and yet only a handful of the scientists were present. The rumor going around the infirmary was that biohazard level four employees had been up all night working on something important. Susan didn't want to believe those two things might be connected, but it was difficult not to.

She was hardly ten feet from the infirmary when she heard a group of nurses discussing Wendy's arrest.

"Have you heard from her?" one asked.

"No," said another. "I was told she and Dr. Dresselhaus had packed up and left the compound."

Only Susan knew different. Wendy and the doctor hadn't left any more than Earl Mullins and his family had. They were somewhere in the basement of Ark Two, at least what was left of them. The thought sickened her and weighed so heavily on her, Susan's legs began to buckle.

"Are you all right?" one of the nurses asked, reaching for her.

Susan straightened. "Yes, I'm fine. I just lost my footing." The nurses were all watching her with concern. "Have any of you seen Autumn?"

"Not since yesterday," replied the one who'd caught Susan. "We got a memo from the director saying we're gonna need all hands on deck for this final immunization."

Susan drew in a deep breath. You didn't need to be a brain surgeon to see that something was off about this next batch. But were the others completely oblivious? Two of the women standing before her were senior nurses. Could they be part of the Ark staff and still be in the dark about what was going on? The disturbing answer seemed to be yes.

With a nod, Susan pushed past them, continuing into the refrigeration room. As she opened the first cooler, Susan couldn't help hoping that she was wrong, that the tiny vials would also read 'placebo' just like the others had. Reaching inside, she plucked one out and studied the label and that was when her heart dropped.

Simian hemorrhagic fever.

Like Ebola or H1N1, whatever this was sounded painful and frightening. A second nurse with another trolley of coolers entered the refrigeration room and Susan tried to hide her concern. The real question was, why would those in charge want to infect civilians seeking shelter in the Ark with a deadly virus?

159

Chapter 33

The security team didn't need to knock twice before Paul sprang up and opened the door. Buck had told him to wait, but it wasn't like they had any other option. No sooner had he flipped the lock and turned the knob than they pushed their way inside, knocking Paul back against the first two bunk beds. He hit them shoulder first and yelped as the wind was knocked from his lungs. Two men in dark blue uniforms came in, followed by Ava Monroe. She glanced around the room. Buck was blocking the computer screen. She raised one black-gloved hand and motioned him to the side. Buck moved a few inches. She did it again. Buck moved another few inches.

0"You can stop this pathetic charade," she told him. "We know what you've been up to. The minute you disabled the bug a silent alarm went off in our security offices. That's my role here, in case you haven't already figured that out. Head of security."

Shoulders slumped, Buck finally stepped aside, revealing the secret documents they'd been going over.

"Should we take them into custody?" the second security officer asked as he removed a pair of handcuffs and stepped forward.

"That won't be necessary," Ava told him, reaching behind her back to produce a four-and-a-half-inch black suppressor which she screwed onto the barrel of the pistol in her other hand.

Paul and Buck looked on with dread.

"That's a SIG Mosquito," Buck said with a hint of admiration.

She grinned and aimed the suppressed pistol at his face. "You know your weapons."

He stepped back. "Well enough to know I don't like 'em being pointed in my direction."

Paul's guts tied into tiny knots.

"Please don't do this," Paul begged, falling to his knees.

"Get on your feet and take it like a man," Buck ordered him.

Both security guards stood between them and Ava. They were surely in a tough spot since any attempt at lunging for her weapon was bound to fail. Paul stopped whining and searched for something he could throw. He was sure Buck was cursing the moment they'd come here.

"Give my regards to the Mullins family," she said and pulled the trigger once, shifted her aim a few feet to the right and pulled it again.

Paul closed his eyes and shuddered. He'd never been shot before and the pain was going to be excruciating.

When he looked up, both guards lay on the floor dead. A trail of smoke rose from the barrel of Ava's pistol.

"Hurry up and hide these bodies," she told Paul and Buck. "We don't have much time."

Chapter 34

Still in shock, Paul followed Ava's instructions. He and Buck stashed the guards' bodies in the bathroom and closed the door.

As they hurried down the corridor, Paul noticed chunks of brain matter in Buck's hair.

"Oh, that's gross," he said, using the sleeve of his tunic to flick them away.

The old man spun. "You better get used to it. I gotta feeling we're about to see a lot more of that."

"Not if I can help it," Ava told them as she led the trio to the elevators and hit the button. An agonizing moment later, it arrived with a ping and they all got on. Ava pulled a keychain from around her neck and inserted a silver key into an opening beneath the digital readout.

"What are you doing?" Paul asked.

"Disabling the cameras and bringing us into the basement."

Buck glanced down and saw that G for 'ground' was the lowest floor. "I don't see any basement."

She grinned. "There's a lot about the Ark you don't know."

A moment later the doors swished open to reveal a concrete tunnel. The space overhead was crammed with pipes and cables.

"This is the guts of the living quarters," she explained. "Temperature control, plumbing. But more importantly, it's where we keep the monitoring equipment for each residence."

"There are cameras too?" Paul asked, doing a quick mental inventory of everything he'd done in the room over the last few days.

Their rubber shoes whisked along the concrete floor as they came up to a nondescript door. Ava flicked through her keys, inserted one and turned. A click sounded and she pushed her way inside. The room was empty of people, but jammed with equipment. A desk ran the length of three walls. Above it was a control panel with bright blinking lights and dozens of monitors.

Paul's jaw dropped open. He approached the screen closest to him for a closer look. A half-naked man was doing pushups and then admiring himself in front of the mirror. In another slice of screen nearby an older woman was sitting on a toilet.

He jerked his eyes away, rubbing them to erase the mental image. "Spying on people in their most private moments. You people are sick, you know that?"

At the other end of the room, Ava was busy typing something into a keyboard.

"What are we doing here?" Buck asked, bewildered by the technological contents of the room.

"Erasing evidence."

Both men understood immediately she was referring to the murder of the two guards.

"I wanted to approach both of you alone, but Van Buren insisted I be accompanied."

"He sent you to get us?" Paul asked.

"To get Buck," she amended, glancing briefly in their direction before her fingers returned to their dance. "They still needed Paul for the concert." She paused and punched the enter key. "There, done. At least now they'll have to check the backup servers to see anything incriminating. Hopefully that'll buy us some time."

Buck's hands were in the air. "Wait just a minute, missy. I'm sure lots of men may be fooled by your good looks, but not me. What do you mean you were coming to get me?"

"I mean sometimes you don't know when to keep your mouth shut and toe the line."

Buck's forearms bunched up with tight cords of muscle.

"She's got a point, Buck," Paul chimed in.

"But how do we know we can trust you?" Buck asked, ignoring Paul's comment.

A nearly imperceptible smile appeared on Ava's lips. "I've been protecting the two of you from the first moment you started causing trouble."

"That was mostly him," Paul said, pointing his finger.

Buck slapped it away. "What do you mean, protecting us?"

"Look, it isn't just you. I've worked hard to make sure no one in the Ark was harmed," Ava told them, her face darkening. "There were many I wasn't able to help, but Paul's history as a famous musician worked in your favor. I was able to convince Van Buren that he could be useful. The note you found under the door…"

"…was you," Buck cut in, putting the pieces together.

"Yes. It was a test."

"A test?" Paul said with exasperation. "It nearly gave me a heart attack."

"You asked how you knew you could trust me, but I needed to know I could trust you."

Paul crossed his arms. "By threatening us?"

"No, I needed to see that you wouldn't stop pushing the limits. I asked you early on if you liked cheesecake, do you remember?"

Paul thought for a moment. "Yeah, and I remember thinking what a strange question it was to ask."

"It was a countersign," Ava said, removing her glasses, "a phrase designed to verify someone's identity. In my case, I ask, 'Do you like cheesecake?' and the other replies, 'I only drive fast cars.'"

"That doesn't make any sense," Paul said, laughing.

She grinned. "It has to be a non sequitur, otherwise the wrong person may say the words by accident. You see, two agents I've never met were supposed to enter the Ark, but they never made it. For a second, I wondered whether the two of you might be the ones I was supposed to make contact with. That was why I asked you the question. But it didn't take long before I realized that neither of you were agent material."

Buck and Paul exchanged wounded looks.

"If anyone here's agent material, it's me, honey," Buck barked back.

"What sort of agency are you talking about anyway?" Paul inquired. "CIA? FBI?"

"Neither," Ava replied. "It's complicated. Let's just say I work for a group that's sworn to stop the Brotherhood's plans for creating a New World Order."

Buck crossed his arms with a satisfied grin. "What did I tell you?" he said, eyeing Paul.

The half-life of Buck gloating over being right was about the same as spent plutonium, which was to say the bragging and grandstanding had only just begun. Paul shook his head in despair.

"So President Perkins…" Buck began.

"Is little more than a lackey," Ava told them. "Placed in the role of Speaker of the House so that once the nukes went off, he could step up and take the helm. All part of the first phase of Project Genesis."

Paul raised an eyebrow. "Genesis. Yeah, we saw a folder on that in the USB you slid under the door."

She nodded and pulled something up on the computer. "As far as ninety-five percent of the people in this installation are concerned, they work for the government. It speaks to the Brotherhood's M.O. They control you without you even knowing it."

"So you're saying they ordered the terrorists to attack their own country?" Paul said with utter disbelief.

Ava shook her head. "No, of course not. These guys are far too slick for something that clumsy. Just like the people working and living in the Ark, the Islamic Liberation Organization was nothing more than another tool. As far as they knew, the funding to pay for the nuclear weapons came from power players in Saudi Arabia. The bombs themselves were channeled to them via Soviet warheads stolen after the Cold War." Ava raised an eyebrow. "Did you really think a group of desert-dwelling terrorists were sophisticated enough to carry out an attack on this scale without a colossal amount of help? You see, the trick was keeping the truth from them. If you hand a gun to a man who wants to kill you, the first thing he'll wonder is whether it's loaded with blanks."

"It's about trust," Buck said.

"Exactly. The ILO doesn't need any incentive to attack the United States. That was never the problem. What they needed was to believe they were acting of their own accord."

167

Paul's head was spinning. It was as though every one of Buck's wacky ideas was coming true at once.

Buck crossed his arms. "Or you coulda saved us all a lot of heartache and put a bullet in Van Buren's head."

"Don't you think I considered that? But if I'd tried to kill him, I would have risked exposing myself. Inevitably someone else would have taken his place and carried out the plan. That's the difference between being brave and being stupid."

"But if all that was phase one of Project Genesis," Paul wondered, "then what's phase two?"

"There's more to tell you, believe me," Ava told him. "You asked before how you knew you could trust me." She swiveled her chair around and punched a key. "What I'm about to show you happened two days ago." Up came a grainy black-and-white video showing a procession of black SUVs entering the bunker's parking area. A dozen men in dark suits then exited and proceeded toward the steel doors.

"Hey, that's President Perkins and his entourage and they aren't wearing any radiation gear," Paul shouted.

As they approached, the doors swung open and the men entered the Ark.

"We were stripped of our clothing," Buck growled. "Put through one indignity after another, not to mention that first shot in my rear end that's still hurting."

Suddenly the lightbulb went off in Paul's head. He looked at Ava, who was staring up at them, waiting for everything to click into place. "What about all the radiation?" he asked, dreading the answer he was sure was about to come.

She shook her head. "The radioactive cloud missed us by about a hundred and fifty miles."

Buck's jaw dropped. "You've got to be kidding me. This whole time they were lying through their teeth."

"They have, but as you'll see it was a lie with a purpose. Inside this compound there is only one other person I can trust. It's someone you know and I've asked them to find Susan and Autumn and bring them here."

"Autumn ran away," Buck told her. "At this point she and Brett could be hiding in one of a million places."

Ava pulled up a black screen with the words ID SEARCH: next to a dialogue box. She typed in *Autumn Edwards* and hit enter. A three-dimensional cutaway of the complex appeared showing a flashing red dot on the third floor of Ark Three.

"How'd you do that?" Buck asked.

"Each of you has been tracked since the moment you arrived. We knew about your visit to the restricted waste management area, which was one of the reasons it became too difficult to protect you any longer."

Buck's hand dropped to his right buttock. "That first shot…"

"… wasn't a shot at all," Ava explained. "It was a chip implant and if you want to stay hidden, we need to remove them right away."

Paul and Buck exchanged an awkward glance.

The old man took a deep breath. "Something tells me I'm not gonna like this one bit."

Chapter 35

When Susan arrived, Buck was bent over the back of a chair with his pants down while Paul was behind him wielding a steel laparoscopic grasper.

She shielded her eyes. "Oh, my goodness."

Paul and Buck straightened right away.

"It's not what you think," Paul stammered, waving the grasper in the air.

Buck reached down to raise his pants, which had fallen around his ankles.

"He's removing a chip," Buck struggled to explain.

Susan nodded. "If you say so."

Ava was stifling a giggle.

Paul turned, searching desperately for support. "Will you tell her?"

Ava's face grew serious as she crossed the room and began explaining the situation. By Susan's side was Craig, Ava's trusted confidant. Paul watched the rollercoaster of emotion as she was filled in. When they were done, he asked about Autumn.

"She's in a restricted area of Ark Three. I couldn't get to her without raising suspicion," Craig said. "Once those chips of yours are out, I'm gonna head back and try again."

"Find Brett Stephens," Susan said. "He's a good boy, I'm sure you'll be able to talk some sense into him."

Ava touched her shoulder. "Brett may be one of them. His orders come from commanding officers who are ultimately loyal to Van Buren. He can't be trusted."

Paul's lingering hope that he would ever see his daughter again was beginning to dwindle. With a heavy heart, he returned to the task at hand.

After the distasteful and somewhat bloody act of removing the tracking devices from each of them was done, Ava placed Buck's and Susan's into a sealed plastic bag and handed it to Craig.

"Drop these in different locations. Might keep them guessing for a while if they begin to search."

"What about mine?" Paul asked.

"The director wants a celebration and the president has asked you to perform." She held up the tiny silver tracking device, no larger than a grain of rice. "We're gonna sew this into your tunic for now. If you need to disappear, simply pull the thread and throw it away."

Buck sat down with a wince of pain. "You still haven't told us about the second phase of Genesis."

"The details are still murky," Ava said, "even for me, but his plan has something to do with the inoculations he's been giving you."

"They were placebos," Susan said, explaining what she'd discovered the day Wendy was taken.

Ava nodded, scratching her chin.

"But then today I was called away to load the vaccine fridge with the inoculations for tomorrow morning and I

171

saw those ones weren't placebos at all, but something called simian hemorrhagic fever."

"Simian hemorrhagic fever?" Paul said, suddenly more terrified than before. "That doesn't sound good at all."

"A weapon his biomed corporation's been working on," Ava informed them, swinging around in her chair, her hands flying over the keyboard. A file came up by the same name along with research results.

Paul scanned over her shoulder. "A three-day incubation period with a sixty-percent mortality rate. I have to say this isn't nearly as deadly as it sounded at first."

"Maybe not," Buck shot back. "But sixty percent of three hundred and thirty million still adds up to a lot of dead people."

"Perhaps the purpose isn't to kill everyone," Paul theorized. "Maybe they just wanna thin the population. Make it harder for everyone to rise up and fight back when the New World Order is put into place."

Buck looked surprised by Paul's insight. "And what better way to keep folks from banding together than filling them with fear about being exposed to a deadly virus?"

"But how exactly do we fit in?" Susan wondered.

Ava looked at each of them. "That part is devilishly simple, I'm afraid. Get the civilians within Ark One accustomed to receiving shots. Then introduce the virus and release them back into the world to spread the virus. It would certainly explain the long incubation period."

Paul ran a sweaty hand through his hair. "So you're saying that in a few days from now, hundreds of human time bombs will be spreading out across the country."

"If that virus gets out," Ava told them, "there won't be a country left."

Chapter 36

Not far from the monitoring station, Ava led Paul, Buck and Susan to what looked like a utility closet. Ten by twenty feet long and lined with three rows of metal shelves, it was a room the two men had become familiar with during their rounds as maintenance workers, a place where they stored extra cleaning supplies, mop heads, buckets and anything else a janitor might need to fulfill his duties. The three of them couldn't help wondering why Ava had brought them here. That was until she yanked one of the shelves away from the wall near the back, spilling bottles of detergent onto the ground as she did so.

A section of gyprock two feet in diameter had been cut and meticulously replaced. She removed the loose piece, set it aside and reached into the dark hole, emerging with a heavy sports bag. Buck moved in to help her, noticing the familiar clanks as they pulled it free from the opening.

Leaning over the bag, Ava unzipped it, revealing an assortment of weapons. Tactical shotguns, M4s, 9mm pistols, even a few MP5 submachine guns.

The concern on Paul's face contrasted with the look of elation on Buck's.

"Where'd a little lady like you get all this sweet firepower?" the old man asked her.

"One piece at a time," she replied. Reaching into the hole, she came out with another bag filled with ammo.

"I'm not sure I like where this is heading," Susan said, cupping her elbows.

"What are you, crazy?" Buck said. "How else do you expect us to blast our way out of here?"

Even Ava was surprised by this.

"You wanna run away?" Paul asked, wondering whether he heard the old man right.

The derisive look on Buck's face made it clear what he was saying. "We didn't start this mess. I'm sure you know where I stand. It's every man for himself in this world."

"Really?" Susan challenged him. "If that were true then where would we be if Ava hadn't been watching our backs?"

Buck's gaze moved to Ava and the disappointed look crinkling her soft features.

"I'll be the first to admit I'd like nothing more than to grab Autumn and get out of here," Paul said. "But this virus business, it changes everything."

Ava's voice was measured. "They're right. Even if you manage to break out, which I doubt, you'd never really be safe. If it wasn't from the fear of simian hemorrhagic fev0er finding you, then it would be the Gestapo-style police under Van Buren's totalitarian regime."

Buck pulled a Benelli shotgun from the pile and stroked the steel-reinforced polymer. There was a fierce debate going on within the old man and it wasn't clear at all which side was winning. At last he replaced the weapon and rose to his feet.

"I didn't come here to be a hero," Buck said. "I got in this mess 'cause I set out to save my family. If they wanna risk their lives on a doomed mission, then so be it, but the first chance I get, I'm outta here."

"Well, that isn't a big surprise," Paul shouted. "You still think of yourself as some kinda lone wolf who doesn't need anyone. What are you gonna do when you get back to your barn and find it's been burned to the ground?"

Buck straightened his shoulders. "I'll cross that bridge when I come to it. No sense worrying about a theoretical event that may never happen." He turned to Ava. "You stuck your neck out for us and for that you have my gratitude. But I didn't cause this mess so I sure as heck ain't gonna clean it up."

And with that Buck spun on his heel and walked away.

"He'll be back," Susan said with a touch of fear and desperation. "The old coot's just being stubborn." Her pleading eyes found Paul. "Right?"

Paul nodded half-heartedly as his father-in-law turned the corner and disappeared. He wanted to offer his wife a glimmer of hope, but something inside told him Buck was gone for good.

Chapter 37

With heavy hearts, they left the utility room a short time later. Paul and Susan each took a Beretta M9A3 pistol along with two additional magazines, hiding them under the waistband of their Ark-issued outfits. The plan for dealing with Van Buren and his objective of infecting the civilians in Ark One was simple. The concert Paul was set to headline this evening would offer a distraction while Susan destroyed the virus being stored at the infirmary and Ava set fire to the biolabs in Ark Two. Of course on paper it sounded fine, but even Ava had to admit that without the explosives her fellow agents were supposed to have provided, she was still unsure how to blow up the labs. Especially since they were the means by which Van Buren could produce more of the virus. A lot of things had to go right for this to work and there wasn't nearly enough time to plan for every eventuality.

And now that Buck had fled the coop, the situation had quickly gone from bad to worse.

The three worked their way down the corridor and toward the elevator.

Once inside, Paul pulled Susan into a tight hug.

"Be careful," he told her, pushing a length of red hair behind her ear.

"I'm not the one about to get on stage to perform for the first time in decades."

The butterflies in his belly stirred. "Good point."

The doors opened and the three of them went in different directions.

Distinctly aware of the pistol under the waistband of his pants, Paul headed for the mess hall. As he drew closer, he caught the sound of musical instruments being sound-checked. Soon, he saw that the entire dining area had been transformed. Tables had been folded in half and pushed up against the walls, which only made his anxiety grow. An improvised stage had been set up. Already civilians and Ark employees alike were beginning to flood in. Within thirty minutes, the mess hall would be packed to the rafters with people who'd been cooped up for days, all eager for an outlet.

"You're late," the guy in a suit barked from on stage. "You practically missed sound check." He flipped through a checklist on his clipboard. "I'm sure I don't need to tell you just about everyone in the Ark will be here tonight."

Paul winked as he walked past him, feeling that old cockiness coming back. "Believe me, I'm counting on it."

As Paul was tuning up his guitar before a growing crowd, Buck was descending into the depths of Ark Three to find Jeb and Allan. The MEP room—mec0hanical, engineering, plumbing—was a particularly impressive array of pipes, levers, valves and boilers. Workers in a mixture of coveralls were busy adjusting, tweaking or in a few cases simply monitoring various gauges. For all of its high-tech beauty, even the guts of a futuristic place like the Ark came down to lengths of copper pipe, boilers and the men who made sure all of it was kept running smoothly. Past this area, Buck came to the generator room and the men who maintained it.

The racket from inside was near deafening as the huge diesel generators worked to provide power.

"It's not a good time, Buck," Jeb said when he saw him. "We lost power from the grid about an hour ago and we've been running off of backup generators."

"Greers Ferry Dam went down?"

"Ain't sure. The juice has come and gone over the last couple days," Jeb yelled over the noise. "I'm sure it'll be back, but the number four generator's been acting up and we're about to shut it down for repairs."

"Believe me, I wouldn't bother you if this wasn't an emergency. But we need to talk."

Jeb bit his lip. "I can give you five minutes."

"That should do. Where's Allan? We'll need him too."

The three men entered a small disheveled office and shut the door. Hanging from a thumbtack on the wall was a calendar of nude women.

Over the course of the next few minutes, Buck laid out exactly what he'd learned. Both men sat in awed silence.

"Are you absolutely sure about this virus business?" Jeb said, rubbing his grease-stained hands together.

Buck nodded. "Would I waste your time coming here if I wasn't?"

"Oh, brother," Allan said. "It's so much worse than we thought."

"So why am I getting the impression you ain't sticking around?" Jeb asked.

"For the simple reason that this mess ain't mine."

The wheels were clearly turning in the back of Allan's head. "There sure are a lot of folks who are gonna die if we do nothing."

"I suggest the two of you take what you need and be ready to hightail it out of here. This is a dog-eat-dog world, gentlemen. You gotta look out for number one."

They didn't seem convinced. "If you say so," Allan said, turning away.

"Hey, if you wanna be heroes then I suggest you go find Craig and offer him your services. You're gonna have to move though, 'cause the situation's about to heat up real soon."

"We just took you for a better man than that," Allan said, not falling for Buck's attempts at misdirection.

Buck's temperature began to rise. "I came out of my way to give you boys a heads-up and this is how you repay me? You may not agree, but I certainly don't need to explain myself to you."

"No, you certainly don't," Jeb said, backing down a little. "What about your family? They going with you?"

Buck shook his head. "I can't help it if they've decided to stick their necks out for a bunch of strangers." His eyes fell so he wouldn't have to see the disappointment in their faces. "Anyway, there's another reason I came. I heard there's a reservoir filled with diesel around here somewhere."

Jeb nodded. "There is. It's what we use to power the generators. Why?"

"Think you can spare some?" Buck asked, not entirely sure they'd still be willing to accommodate his request, not after all this.

"How much you need?" Jeb asked, looking uncertain.

"About enough to fill the tank of a Hummer."

Chapter 38

Approaching the infirmary, Susan did her best to ignore the anxiety building up in her fingers and toes, a feeling that migrated up her spine and drew her scalp tight against the top of her head once she was inside. One of the few nurses left on duty was bandaging a child's foot.

"How come you're not at the concert?" the nurse asked with a touch of incredulity.

Susan tried to laugh and could only hope it didn't sound too forced. "I forgot something."

The nurse nodded and smiled, but something about the way her eyes traced Susan's path toward the back of the infirmary made Susan even more uneasy.

She still wasn't clear how to destroy the vials of simian hemorrhagic fever, especially without exposing herself to the deadly pathogen. Unlike other hospitals, the infirmary didn't have an incinerator where old medication and biohazardous materials could be disposed of. No, that would have made her life far too easy. She also couldn't exactly pack the vials up and cart them off, not without being spotted and arrested, or worse.

In the infirmary's tiny lunch room next to the coffee machine was a metal trash bin. Susan removed the trash bag and carried the metal can to the refrigeration area. If she couldn't bring the virus to an incinerator, then she'd just have to bring the incinerator to the virus. Along the way, she opened up a cupboard the nurses used to store tongue depressors and bandages and scooped out four bottles of rubbing alcohol. In a lower cupboard was a pack of matches nurses kept for relieving the pressure from smashed fingers. In particularly bad cases blood tended to collect beneath the nail and the only way to relieve the pain was to heat a paperclip and burn through the nail itself.

Armed with these items, she hurried into the refrigeration room, careful not to be seen. Although she hadn't spotted anyone else, it wasn't unthinkable that at least one other nurse might be on duty. She began by opening each of the fridge doors, grabbing handfuls of vials and depositing them into the trash can. The fire would surely trigger an alarm, but by then she hoped to be long gone. After the third and final fridge was empty, Susan opened each of the bottles of rubbing alcohol and poured them over the vials. She was on her last bottle when a knock came at the door.

"Susan, you in there?"

It was the nurse from before. Beverly was her name. Or was it Brittany?

"Just a minute," Susan called out. In two strides she was at the door, opening it a crack, ready to fend off the nosy nurse with assurances that everything was all right.

So long, that was, as the nurse didn't spot the trash can behind her or the overpowering odor of rubbing alcohol.

But Beverly or Brittany wasn't alone. There were two Ark security personnel only steps behind her. The nurse's eyes narrowed. With a quick slide of her foot, the nurse stuck her leg out to keep the door from closing.

Susan responded by slamming her open palm square in the middle of her chest. The nurse went reeling backwards, falling into a tray of medical instruments. Metal clattered to the floor as Susan slammed the door and fumbled for the lock. But to her horror she realized there wasn't any lock. In another three seconds the guards would be inside and on top of her.

The matches were on the counter behind her and Susan lunged for them, her fingers shaking as she peeled back the cover and peeled off one of the paper sticks. That was when the door swung open and the guards froze for a moment, their eyes moving between the trash can and the matches in her hand. Terror bubbling inside of her, Susan struggled to swipe the matchstick against the strike strip. A single flame was all she needed to destroy this batch of the virus.

And in that instant, fate displayed her temperamental nature once again as the match failed to light and the guards tackled Susan to the ground.

Chapter 39

Van Buren was walking through the atrium of Ark Three on his way to the tram when a Secret Service agent stopped him.

"What is it?" the director barked impatiently. "The celebration's already begun in the mess hall of Ark One and I'm late. This better be important."

"One of the civilians was caught trying to destroy the vaccines we're issuing tomorrow."

Van Buren bit his bottom lip. "How far did they get?"

"It was a woman and we caught her in time, sir," the agent told him.

"Where's she being held?"

"Interrogation room, security headquarters."

0"I trust you've notified Ms. Monroe and removed the vials to a safe location."

"The vials are safe, but we can't get a hold of Ms. Monroe."

The last time Van Buren had spoken to her she'd been heading over to arrest a civilian troublemaker. He wondered if something terrible had befallen her.

"Where's the individual she took into custody?"

The agent shook his head. "We don't know that either."

"Use his biochip to track him and find out. When I'm back, I'll have a word with our little saboteur." Van Buren went to walk away.

"Sir, there's one more thing."

The director sighed and skidded to a stop.

"Someone's opened the airlock in Ark Two." The agent held up a tablet which showed a three-dimensional schematic of the facility. A growing swarm of tiny dots were moving over the main floor.

"What is this?" Van Buren asked.

"The animals, sir. Someone let them out."

The elevator doors opened onto biohazard level four and Ava caught sight of the guard seated at the end of the corridor. Past that door was a changing room where scientists donned the suits they needed to work in such a hazardous environment. With most, if not all, of the Ark personnel at the concert, Ava hoped no one would need to get hurt. No one except for this guard.

As he stood to greet her, Ava pulled a pistol from behind her back and double-tapped two rounds into the guard's forehead. His body slumped back into the chair, his eyes open and staring at the ceiling. She felt for a pulse and then closed his eyes.

The sound of the elevator doors opening behind her made her spin. Over the barrel of her pistol, a man emerged from the shadow. He was carrying something heavy.

"Whoa," he said, raising his free hand. "Don't shoot."

"The heck are you doing here?" she asked, more annoyed than anything.

A slow grin formed on Buck's face. "And miss out on all the fun?" He lifted the large canister a few inches. "I brought drinks."

The two of them entered the change room and suited up. Destroying the lab would also mean entering the lair of some of the deadliest viruses and bacteria on the planet.

"You know that diesel you brought won't explode like gasoline."

Buck smiled. "Not like gas, but it'll burn and it's oily, which will make it next to impossible for the sprinkler system to put it out."

Ava entered a code in the keypad and they entered the hot zone.

"Looks like everyone's on vacation," Buck said. The heavy suit made it difficult to talk.

Along the walls were glass enclosures where scientists could observe and manipulate the genetic structure of the various pathogens.

Nearby were a number of walk-in fridges and freezers where specimens were kept in cold storage. A row of animal cages stood empty.

Buck tapped her on the shoulder. "What would you have done if I hadn't showed up?"

"This," she said, turning on the gas to a Bunsen burner. "Start spreading that diesel around nice and even."

Buck opened the fridges and freezers, pouring the fuel liberally inside. Before long the entire room was coated. At the other end, Ava opened a burner and lit the flame, turning it on high. It wouldn't be long before the natural gas from one end of the room migrated to the other and when it did, she wanted to make sure they had both reached a safe distance.

Hurrying to the change room, they helped each other out of their suits and fled down the corridor to the elevator.

If Susan was also successful in her mission, then in a matter of minutes, the virus would be no more. The final surprise Ava had left in Craig's hands. It should be going off any minute.

Chapter 40

Over in the mess hall, Paul was struggling to catch his groove. It hadn't taken long for the audience to fill every conceivable space. That he'd never played a single lick with his bandmates before this evening wasn't the worst of it. Nor was it the Beretta he'd secretly taped to the back of his guitar, the same pistol that was currently digging into his ribs. What was throwing him off was the lyrics to his own songs. They were coming to him barely a split second before he was supposed to be belting them out and on more than one occasion he'd forgotten an entire section, improvising with anything he could, sometimes even gibberish. His former agent Larry Sanders, a fat and balding workaholic and perfectionist, would have been appalled.

The only thing helping Paul was the projection screen they'd mounted behind him, flashing images of women showing off oversized shoulder pads and bad eighties hair. The good news was the band was at least vaguely familiar with each of his songs and with every one they played, they got a little bit better.

Slowly, Paul started to settle down and as he did, a strange thing began to happen. He found himself having fun. At one point during the chorus of *Take Me All the Way*, the audience swaying back and forth, some even reciting the lyrics, he hopped up and down, swinging his arm like a windmill. The crowd went wild and so too did Paul when he felt the pistol starting to come loose. The jumping and chafing against his belly must have peeled the tape back and now he was forced to keep his guitar pulled tight against his torso or risk the gun falling and skittering across the stage.

The crowd quieted down. Paul continued to hit the notes hard, but people weren't even looking at him anymore. They were staring behind him and many of their mouths were moving, but not like they were singing along—they were reading something.

He peered over his shoulder as the other band members did the same. The ladies in horrible clothes were gone. Scrolling across the canvas projector screen in their place was a series of words. Even the music had died down as all of them read along.

The director has lied to you. There is no radiation. There is no sanctuary. Your lives are in danger. Tomorrow morning all civilians will be infected with a lethal virus and sent out to spread death throughout what's left of the country.

Even the radiation readouts on the walls were displaying the same message.

Then came a distant explosion and all hell broke loose.

Chapter 41

Ava had just destroyed the lab. That was Paul's first thought as the mess hall shook and the lights dimmed and then came back on.

Shouts of fear emanated from the crowd as civilians and Ark personnel alike began to panic. Guards and soldiers positioned near each of the three major exits attempted to prevent the audience from panicking. A military officer stationed behind the front lines fired his pistol into the air to regain control, which only made things worse, transforming a panic into a stampede. Perhaps thinking they'd been fired on, guards and soldiers at each exit began firing indiscriminately. Civilians and Ark personnel were cut down right where the0y stood. Others dove for cover. Seeing the carnage, Paul grabbed his pistol and extra magazines and dropped his guitar onto the stage. Nearby, his other bandmates ducked behind speakers and amplifiers.

Innocent people were getting slaughtered and Paul had to do something to help them. A guard less than ten yards away dropped to one knee as he frantically tried to reload his MP7A1 submachine gun. Paul leveled his pistol and fired off three rounds in quick succession. All three missed the guard, punching holes in the floor and wall around his target. Paul had just lost the element of surprise and given away his position. Not a great start.

The guard punched his magazine in and raised his weapon. Without taking care to aim, Paul emptied the remaining rounds from his Beretta. Two struck home, one hitting the guard in the abdomen, the other in the neck. He dropped his weapon at once, clutching the wound at his throat as blood ran between his fingers. Adrenaline pumping through his veins, Paul couldn't yet feel the full implication of what he'd just done.

A soldier nearby made a rapid analysis of the situation and spotted Paul. The second magazine was in Paul's waistband and he reached for it, knowing he wouldn't have enough time before he was shot dead.

The muzzle of the soldier's gun rose and was nearly even with Paul when a loud boom threw the soldier forward. He fell to the ground without moving. More violent gunfire came from that same direction. The people around them screamed and in some cases fell from bullet wounds. A battle was raging around the corner, but Paul couldn't see what was happening.

He reloaded his pistol and moved to reposition himself. Before he had a chance, the gunfire stopped and men wearing dirty civilian clothing and wielding an assortment of firearms appeared. At the helm was Jeb, then Allan and a host of other men with grease-stained faces. Bringing up the rear were Craig, Ava and a face Paul had thought he might never see again. Buck. They were waving groups of civilians over, ushering them out of the way and to safety.

But that wasn't entirely right, was it? They weren't just moving them to the rear. Other resistance members in the rear armed as many people in beige clothing as they could.

This was no longer a sophisticated jailbreak, it was a full-scale revolution.

Chapter 42

"What's happening?" Autumn asked, fearful.

"I'm not sure," Brett replied honestly.

The two of them were in the soldiers' barracks on the third floor of Ark Three. Only seconds before they'd heard an explosion and felt the ground at their feet tremble. Two floors up was the command center for the entire Ark. From there they might figure out what was happening. Reaching out, Brett took Autumn's hand and led her away.

When she'd come the day before, telling him her parents were trying to leave and wanted to take her with them, Brett had felt this was the safest place for her to be. To access this floor, a civilian without clearance would need to get through security in the atrium, an elevator locked with a password-protected keypad and finally a barracks filled with guards at one end and soldiers at the other.

As far as the explosion went, Brett could only hope it was some kind of accident and that it would quickly be under control. Instead of taking the elevator, he led her up via the stairs. No sooner had they opened the push door leading to the emergency exit than government personnel streamed down.

"What's going on?" he shouted.

"There's been an explosion," an older man in a dark blue suit yelled.

Still wondering whether or not the detonation had been an accident, Brett thought of his rifle. It was back in the barracks. The 9mm service pistol on his hip would have to do. Holding Autumn's hand tightly, Brett pushed through the river of humanity. He knew better than to be like all the other lemmings when the stuff hit the fan. Intel was your friend, and they needed to find out what was going on.

At last they fought their way up the two stories and came out next to the command center. Two soldiers were posted there with M4s. Brett showed his ID and he and Autumn began to head inside. They moved to stop them before Brett said, "She's with me, it's okay."

Reluctantly, they stood down. The situation was obviously more chaotic than he'd previously thought. Inside, a tiny group of commanders and politicians were arguing over what to do while phones at empty desks overlooking the bank of giant screens were ringing off the hook. Normally there were at least thirty people manning the various stations here. Right now there were five.

Eyes wide, Autumn stared up at a bank of screens and pointed.

Brett followed her gaze and saw what had horrified her. In one, flames were shooting up the elevator shaft and into the atrium in Ark Two. The screens showing biohazard levels three and four were black. On two, the fire from the lower floors was starting to break through the floor. If it wasn't contained, Ark Two would be completely lost.

Another screen showed the atrium downstairs, with people running frantically, dodging cats and dogs and a dizzying array of animals, presumably escapees from the Park.

Then Brett caught the final screen and saw the heated firefight in the mess hall. His fellow brothers in arms were being overrun by a ragtag group of civilians. As each soldier fell, his weapons were snatched by a man or woman in beige. The sight didn't simply shock him, it ripped his guts out and threw them on the floor. He was torn between protecting Autumn and racing to help his friends and comrades. His indecision couldn't have lasted for more than a second when a voice shouted from the other end of the command center.

"There you are," it said. "If you only knew how long we've been looking for you."

"Mom," Autumn shouted.

Coming toward them were Van Buren, three members of the Secret Service detail that protected him, and Autumn's mother, Susan.

"These two are both going to be taught a lesson. Now bring the daughter," Van Buren ordered, waving his hand with all the parental authority of a man calling a child to come in from playing outside.

Brett's muscles grew tense. Beside him, Autumn's expression morphed from fear to terror.

Van Buren and his entourage had swung around, but now they stopped.

"Are you hard of hearing, soldier? I gave you an order."

No one was going to teach Autumn a lesson.

Brett whispered to Autumn, "When I give the word, I want you to run for those doors and not look back no matter what happens."

"What are you gonna do?"

"Go down there and get her," Van Buren told his men.

"Ready? Now," Brett shouted and pulled his pistol, firing off at least five shots, aiming at the Secret Service agents heading his way.

The one closest to him rolled down a set of shallow steps and popped up with his own pistol drawn. Autumn pushed through the door right as Brett was struck by what felt like a sledgehammer in the chest. It knocked the wind out of him and threw him instantly to the floor. The gun hit the floor and skidded away.

The agents arrived and kicked his pistol out of reach. But they didn't run after Autumn. They didn't need to. One of the guards stationed at the door had her over his shoulder. She kicked and screamed harder when she saw Brett lying there. He had enough time to see her face one last time before the final shot.

Chapter 43

The battle in the mess hall was still in full swing when Paul linked up with Buck and Ava. Civilians armed with pistols, shotguns and rifles surged forward. Soon, facing sheer force of numbers, the soldiers and Ark security teams holding the line broke and ran.

"Has your man found Autumn yet?" Paul asked, searching Ava's face for good news.

Craig came up beside them, a growing patch of blood on his right leg. "She's been taken by Van Buren," he said.

Down the other two corridors, bursts of muffled gunfire could still be heard as they fled.

"And there's more," Craig said. "Susan was captured before she could complete her mission."

Paul felt the world spinning away from him. Buck reached out to hold him in place.

Now Jeb and Allan were heading their way. "We got 'em on the run, boys," he said and let out something that sounded like a rebel yell.

As Paul glanced around the mess hall at the dead and wounded, it hardly seemed a reason to celebrate. Some of the nurses were already attending to those in need of help. One of them came to Craig and looked at his leg. "I'll be fine," he told her. "There are others in far worse shape."

Addressing Jeb and Allan, Ava said, "I need you and your men from the generator rooms to open the bunker doors and get the women and children out." She handed him a slip of paper with two codes. "The first should open the steel doors. The second is the emergency code in case they've sealed the exits."

Jeb nodded as he and Allan left.

Paul removed the magazine from his pistol and checked to see how many rounds he had left. "Can you still track Autumn's whereabouts?" he asked Craig.

"Ark Three, top floor," he replied.

"Forget heading there by tram," Buck said. "By now most of Ark Two's probably in flames. Best to head through the Park."

They reached Ark Three and came under fire as soon as they exited the airlock. Buck charged in first, laying down an impressive volley with the AA-12 automatic shotgun he was carrying. Ava, Paul and Craig quickly followed suit. This area would be the linchpin since it led to the blast doors and the parking area beyond. Already, streams of Ark employees were fleeing the battle. Van Buren's men didn't seem to care, however, and they fired through the groups in the hopes of making a lucky hit.

198

The bulk of the opposition in the Atrium was coming from a group of guards sheltered behind the security desk. Every few seconds, one of them would pop his head out and squeeze off a few rounds and whenever they did, Buck responded with a burst from his shotgun. The sound of the weapon was scary enough, not to mention the noise the buckshot made as it slammed into the desk and wall beyond. The guards were pinned down, which gave Paul and the others the opportunity to circle around.

When they reached the desk, Ava was the one to do the deed and cut the men down with her SIG. Now the only sound came from the scattered groups of people trying to escape.

"This way," Craig said, urging them toward the bank of elevators.

They scrambled inside, Ava punching the access code before the doors slid shut.

They would have about a minute to check their ammo and reload weapons before they reached the tenth floor, except for Buck, whose auto shotgun held a hundred rounds.

Soft music played.

"That Neil Diamond?" Paul asked.

"*Sweet Caroline*," Buck grunted.

Paul racked the slide on his pistol, chambering a round. Craig checked the tablet.

"Head right," he instructed them. "Third door on the left."

"That's Van Buren's office," Ava said, concerned.

With a gentle ping, the elevator swooshed open. The hallway vibrated with flashing red emergency lights, making it hard to see. One by one, they moved out, scanning both sides as they did.

"Clear," Ava called out.

Buck looked left. "Clear."

Slowly they worked their way down the corridor. There was no one within sight, no guards or government types in suits pleading to be spared. Papers scattered on the ground spoke of people fleeing in a great hurry.

"Through here," Craig whispered, pointing.

Buck stepped forward and planted his foot next to the handle, kicking open the door, revealing the room where Van Buren's secretary sat, but it wasn't empty. Inside were three Secret Service agents. Two of them were loading weapons and the third was stuffing gold and silver coins into a knapsack.

Startled, the three agents moved to raise their weapons, but Buck got there first. Three thunderous blasts and each of them was thrown back, falling to the floor dead.

A pair of mahogany double doors led to Van Buren's office and the four of them pushed their way inside. In the center of the room, two stretchers were laid out. Autumn lay in the left, Susan in the right. They were both strapped down with terrified expressions. Van Buren was holding a syringe in the side of Susan's neck, his thumb on the depressor.

"Drop your weapons at once," Van Buren shouted, "or I'll pump her full of this stuff."

Shooting the director from here risked hitting one or both of the women. More importantly, there wasn't any guarantee doing so would prevent him from emptying that syringe.

While Buck laid his shotgun on the table and Ava and Craig did the same with their own weapons, Paul had slipped his pistol under his waistband.

"Your sleight of hand needs work, Mr. Edwards. I won't ask you again." Van Buren jiggled the needle in Susan's neck and she screamed.

"Okay, okay," Paul said, putting the gun on the table and raising his hands. He hoped Ava or Buck still had a weapon on them. With no better options, they would have to play along for now.

Van Buren sneered. "I saw the message you sent to the other bunkers ordering them to destroy their copies of the virus," he told Ava. "Very clever. I won't even ask why. I thought you understood what we were doing here, thought you had vision and the guts to do what was needed, but I see now that I was wrong."

Another door opened behind Van Buren and President Perkins walked in wielding a machete. The director grinned when he saw him.

"Did you bring the biosuit?"

"Of course," Perkins said, eyeing the four at the other end of the room.

"You're going to infect Susan and put her in that suit, aren't you?" Ava said, her hand inching toward her gun on the table.

"Nonsense," he said. "These two lovely ladies are our tickets out of here. Do as you're told and we'll let them go when we've reached a safe distance."

He was lying and even Paul could see that.

"Go collect their weapons," he told Perkins.

Buck stirred and Paul felt a chill run up his spine. The old man wasn't going to let that happen. Losing their guns was tantamount to a death sentence. None of them were that stupid.

Perkins was passing behind Van Buren when two things happened in rapid succession.

Buck pulled out a hidden pistol.

Perkins raised his machete and brought it down, slicing off Van Buren's right hand at the wrist.

The director's face became a mask of horror as he stared down in disbelief, blood pumping onto the floor at his feet from his severed limb. In a desperate act of self-preservation, he screamed, clutching the stump to his chest to stop the bleeding before falling backwards.

Perkins plucked the needle from Susan's neck. He then looked directly at Ava.

"Why'd you do it?" she asked.

"For one simple reason," he told her. "I like fast cars."

And a light went on in Paul's head. Perkins was one of the two agents Ava had been waiting for.

The syringe was still in Perkins' hand as Buck, Paul and the others rushed over to untie the women. When Perkins held it up to the light, his face began to darken.

"I think we have a problem," he said, as Van Buren continued to moan in agony behind him.

"What is it?" Paul asked, helping Autumn to her feet.

Perkins showed him the needle. Most of the liquid inside was gone. Paul turned to his wife and then to the others.

"What is it?" Susan asked in a panicked voice, pressing her hand against the side of her neck.

"Some of the virus might have got into you," Paul told her. He turned to Ava. "What do we do? Isn't there a cure?"

From the floor, Van Buren was making strange noises that sounded to Paul a lot like laughter. "There was," he said in a barely audible whisper. "But you destroyed it when you blew up the labs."

Paul turned to Buck and Ava, who both shook their heads.

"We didn't know," Buck said, oozing guilt and remorse.

Van Buren was still laughing when Paul snatched his pistol off the table and emptied it into him.

Autumn's hands clamped over her ears as she cried. The others stared on in surprise. Not because the man hadn't deserved it, more that Paul had been the one to do the deed. He was still clutching the pistol, the slide all the way back, when Buck pushed his hands down.

"Come," the old man said. "We need to get Susan into the suit. Keep the virus from spreading."

Paul dropped the pistol and turned to his wife. Tears were rolling down her cheeks as her feet were being fed in one at a time. He'd seen the stats on simian hemorrhagic fever just like the rest of them had. Susan had a forty percent chance of pulling through this.

As the zipper was pulled closed, her face distorted by the plastic visor, he squeezed her hand and told her how much he loved her.

Chapter 44

By the time they made it out of the bunker and into the underground parking area, the streams fleeing the facility had dwindled to a trickle. Thankfully, the Hummer was still in the same spot where Susan had first left it.

Carefully, they emptied out the rear cargo hold and loaded Susan inside, making sure to keep her propped up and comfortable. On the way down, Paul had made the mistake of asking where Brett was. His daughter had burst into tears and was still crying as she lifted herself into the back seat of the Hummer and fastened her seat belt.

With no sign of Jeb, Allan or the rest of his crew, Paul could only hope that they'd made it out safely.

"Well, I guess this is it," Buck said, one clenched fist perched against his hip in a careless manner. He was trying hard to convince Ava he wasn't sad to see her go, but Paul was sure no one was buying into his tricks.

Next to her was Perkins, his suit caked with Van Buren's blood. The mystery of the second missing secret agent had also been revealed. He had been posing as Perkins' assistant, a man killed during the detonation in Baltimore harbor.

"Are you sure you'll have enough fuel?" she asked.

Buck pointed to an eighteen-wheeler parked a hundred feet away. "I'll top her up by syphoning from that transport truck." He paused. "Which way are the two of you headed?"

"Not sure yet," Ava told him, rubbing her palms against her legs. "First thing is to make contact with our headquarters and let them know the virus has been neutralized. After that we'll await further orders."

"You do have a man in high office now," Paul said. "That's gotta be worth something."

Perkins smiled. "I hope it is."

"I just wish you'd put a stop to Van Buren before things spun so far out of control," Buck said.

"There was a window to act and we missed it," Perkins explained, or at least tried to. "Even in my organization, there's a bureaucracy that stifles an agent's freedom of action."

Buck didn't seem to be buying it, but Paul was in no mood to leave on bad terms.

"I'd ask for your phone number," Buck said to Ava. "But something tells me it'll be a while before phones of any kind are up and running again."

"I read your file," she said with a wink. "I know where to find you."

They parted ways then, Buck watching as Ava and Perkins disappeared back into the Ark.

The stop to fill the fuel tank and jerry cans was quicker than expected and before they knew it, they were heading outside.

Emerging from the underground parking, they were struck at once by piercing rays of early-morning sunshine.

"You don't trust them, do you, Buck?" Paul asked, as the Hummer rolled out of Sugarloaf Mountain and onto the pontoon bridge.

"I don't trust anyone," he replied matter-of-factly. "You know that. But it wouldn't surprise me one bit to know they'd purposely held back from taking out Van Buren and his people sooner."

"For what reason?"

"Let the Brotherhood do all the dirty work, that's why. That way they could come along and scoop the country up for a rock-bottom price after it was all shot to hell."

Paul glanced back at Susan to make sure she was okay. Through the back window, he watched the mountain shrinking into the distance. He couldn't have been happier to see it go.

Chapter 45

The sights they encountered on the rest of the journey home were distressing, to say the least. Highways pockmarked with abandoned cars. Dead bodies scattered along the road, their bones picked over by crows and other wild animals. It wouldn't be too much longer before nature reclaimed what was left of the country.

Paul still wasn't sure what to make of Buck's suggestion that the secret organization Ava worked for had failed to prevent the country's downfall. It certainly didn't bode well and yet, given the choice, he would gladly take Perkins' stewardship over Van Buren's and for one simple reason. Perkins' valiant attempt to save Susan had demonstrated the one character trait Van Buren had sorely lacked: empathy.

They were less than three miles from home when Susan died. Her symptoms had started that first evening—much earlier than expected—and within twenty-four hours, her chances for recovery had gone from decent to grim.

Her body was buried beside the barn on Buck's property. Afterward, they'd each taken turns reciting a prayer, Paul wondering the whole way through where he would find the strength to carry on. But the answer was clear and standing on either side of him.

Following an inspection of both properties, they soon discovered that both homes had been looted during their absence. For now it was safer if they stayed in Buck's bunker, although next to the Ark it felt positively microscopic. Still, for the first time in a while, Paul and Autumn truly felt safe.

With time on his hands, Paul couldn't stop his mind from spinning in all kinds of directions. Many of those thoughts centered around the devastating impact of Susan's death. The Brits often used 'gutted' to describe a sense of deep despair and that was exactly how he felt.

When he wasn't trying to remember the sound of his wife's voice, he was busy thinking about what was left of the country.

No doubt about it, America had been irrevocably transformed as a consequence of the attacks and by forces far greater than anything which had shaped her during all her past wars combined. It was a rather ironic twist that borne from that loss and tragedy came an opportunity to rebuild. To do things better than they had in the past. To create a place where life, liberty and the pursuit of happiness weren't only words on an aging piece of parchment. They were emblazoned with a renewed sense of meaning.

Paul knew Susan would have agreed.